Penelope's Pearls
Book five in the Clover Creek Caravan Series
Kirsten Osbourne

A note to readers: Several of my early readers were confused by my use of the word receipt instead of recipe. Receipt is the word that was in common use until roughly the beginning of the 20th century. In past books I have used the word recipe to keep from being confusing, but it bothered me, so I changed it in this one.

In my little town in Idaho (Montpelier) there is an Oregon Trail Center which has had an entire library donated from a deceased professor's possessions. All the books are on American history, and a good deal of them are on the Oregon Trail. I'm the librarian, and I spend as much time reading the books as I do cataloging them. I hope my research shows as you read this book. Enjoy!

Chapter One

Thursday, May 27th, 1852

Today was a very trying day for me. We had journeyed only two miles when I broke a wagon wheel. I was ready to give up and sit on the side of the road weeping, wondering how I had ever thought I could make the drive to Oregon completely alone.

But as usual, the kind Mr. Jensen stopped and helped me. Well, the whole company stopped, and I put us behind schedule, but no one seemed to hold it against me. I'm so thankful the company has new captains because Mr. Bedwell would have left me alone there and gone on. He made no secret of the fact that he didn't think a woman could or should make this journey alone. I disagree with him...usually. I didn't for a while this morning though.

To thank Mr. Jensen for stopping to help me, I've invited him to partake of the supper I make this evening. I'm not certain it's a good idea, because it will mean we're alone—within plain sight of others—for a good long while. Mr. Jensen doesn't seem to speak much, so it will be up to me to carry the conversation. I'm sure I'll make it work, but it won't be the most pleasant experience I've ever had.

I am thankful he helped me and has so many other times. I feel indebted to him, and it's not a feeling I like. I've offered to pay him for his help, but he won't hear of it. A home-cooked meal is all he wants. I have to wonder if he knows I've cooked very little in my life before our journey west. Hopefully, he'll be satisfied with my meal.

After the long drive that day, Penelope let Mr. Jensen see to her animals as he always did for her, and then she started the fire. She didn't know how she'd make it without the kind man helping her every step of the way. She'd promised herself before leaving Virginia that she wouldn't be beholden to anyone on this trip, and here she was, owing the blacksmith so much more than a simple meal.

She started a simple meal she'd learned to make along the way—johnny cakes and bacon. As soon as it was ready, she put it onto two plates and poured them each a cup of cold coffee from the pot she'd made that morning. She only hoped he'd be happy with cold coffee, because she had no idea what he drank. She did know the doctor insisted on drinking coffee and not water, but no one knew why, other than people who were coffee drinkers were less likely to get cholera.

When he joined her a few minutes later, he took his cap off in her presence, reminding her of the men in Virginia who had always shown her the respect her father insisted she deserved. "It's just johnny cakes and bacon," she said softly. She watched his face carefully for a sign of contempt, but there was nothing.

"It sounds wonderful," he said, taking a seat on a rock beside the fire pit that had been formed long before by other travelers on their way to Oregon.

Penelope handed him a plate. "I'm learning to cook, but I'm not the best yet, so if you can't eat it let me know, and I'll make something else." She wanted to please him with the meal for all the help he'd given her along the way. She just wished there was something more she could do to thank him.

He took a bite and smiled. "It's good. Only thing that would make it better would be honey or jam."

She jumped up and went to the back of her wagon, finding a small jar of honey she'd purchased back in Independence but hadn't tried yet. She wasn't sure why she hadn't broken into it when honey was one of her very favorite things, but at that moment, she was happy to have something to offer him.

"Here you go," she said handing it to him.

Mr. Jensen smiled big and accepted it from her, pouring a bit over his johnny cakes and then handing the honey to her. "You'll like it this way. I promise."

Penelope gladly accepted and poured a small amount onto her plate. "I'm sure I'll love it. I just wish I'd been the one to think of it." She took a bite and smiled. "This makes it a lot better!"

"Thank you for inviting me to eat with you this evening," he said softly. His dark eyes seemed to be saying so much more, but she couldn't fathom what.

"It's the least I could do after all you've done for me. I was determined to do it all myself and you came along and made everything so much easier for me. I appreciate all you do."

"I'm happy to do what I can to make your journey easier. I wish you'd let me do more." His voice was earnest, and she knew that he meant every word he said. He wanted to do more for her.

"What more could you do?" she asked. "You already feed and water my oxen, hitch them in the morning, unhitch them in the afternoon, and you make sure my wagon is in working order. I can't imagine what more *anyone* could do for me."

"I could set your tent up for you in the evenings, and then take it down in the mornings."

She shook her head adamantly. "I enjoy sleeping under the stars any night it's not raining. And when it is raining, I have no problem climbing into the back of my wagon. Buying that tent was a silly luxury I don't really need." She wished she'd saved her money and the room in the back of the wagon, but it was too late now unless she wanted to leave it on the side of the trail. She didn't like how the entire trail seemed littered with emigrants' possessions though, and she had no desire to add to them.

He sighed. "You're going to be stubborn about this, aren't you, Miss Brainerd?"

"I'm stubborn about a lot of things," she responded. "It's what makes me who I am." She couldn't count the number of times her father had called her stubborn. She almost saw it as a compliment.

"You seem nervous about something," he said a short while later, when his plate had been cleaned. "Like you're always watching over your shoulder."

"May I confide in you, Mr. Jensen?" she asked.

"Only if you'll call me Herb."

Herb. It must be short for Herbert, she thought. "All right, Herb. I left my family's plantation without telling anyone where I was going. You see, I'm against slavery, and speaking those words aloud always made my father angry." He'd threatened to whip her if she ever said them again, so she'd held her tongue and bided her time until she was ready to leave.

"Did your family own slaves?" he asked.

She nodded. "Hundreds of them."

"And you left all that behind to travel west by yourself?" He seemed dumbfounded by her decision, and she knew it was one not many women would have made.

Penelope shrugged. "I do have the whole company as traveling companions."

"But no man to protect you."

She frowned at him, narrowing her eyes. "I have the safety of the whole company with me. I don't need a man to watch over me." The very idea of having a man turned her stomach a little. The man she'd been affianced to had been nothing short of evil.

Herb nodded, but he seemed reluctant. "All right."

"You don't think that's enough, do you?"

"I don't know for sure, but I worry about people like Bedwell out and about at night with you all alone."

Penelope nodded. "Of all the men in this camp, he's the one who worries me the most." She thought for a minute about telling him about how terrible it had been when they'd both accepted a supper invitation from the Bentleys, but she didn't want him to know about it. She worried that he might take his protective nature a little too far if he found out.

Herb leaned forward. "I know you only invited me to have supper with you because you're grateful for my help, but I have a proposal."

Penelope closed her eyes and said a silent prayer that he wasn't about to ask her to marry him. She knew that everyone seemed to get married quickly on the trail, but that wasn't something she wanted.

"Let's pretend we're courting, and then everyone will assume that you have my protection." His voice was soft and deep, and the very idea seemed to permeate the air around them.

She opened her eyes, intrigued by the offer. "What do you get out of this arrangement?"

"I know that you'll be safer. Hopefully, a meal now and then."

She bit her lip, considering. "If you don't mind that you'll be getting my inept cooking, I would agree to cook for you every night. I'd need you to give me a portion of your food stores, but I really don't mind cooking. It's no harder to cook for two than it is for one."

He smiled. "I like that idea."

"What would this courting you're proposing entail? I don't want to be kissing you in front of others or anything like that." She'd never been kissed, and she didn't want her first kiss to be a fake one for others' benefit. And she wasn't sure yet how she would feel about kissing Herb. He was good to her, and that made him very attractive in her eyes, but kissing? It seemed terribly intimate.

"It wouldn't be kissing. I think I'd ask you to walk with me in the evenings after supper. We both need the exercise after driving all day. Perhaps you could take my arm and make it look more authentic, and then meals with you. Nothing more."

"I think that would work nicely." Penelope smiled at him. She would feel safer if people thought she had the protection of a man. It was in direct contrast to what she'd just been thinking, but she couldn't let that bother her.

"Good. Then that's what we'll do." He set his plate down. "Would you care to walk with me, Miss Brainerd?"

"If we're going to be courting, you'll have to call me Penelope," she said with a grin. "Let me just take care of the dishes, and I'll be ready to go."

She'd never in her life touched a dirty dish until she'd run away to go on the trail, but she had learned quickly how to do the dreadful chore, and she made short work of the task. When she was finished and the dishes were stowed away in the back of her wagon until morning, she walked to Herb's side. "Let's take that walk now," she said, taking his arm.

As they walked through camp in the direction they'd traveled that day, Penelope was aware that every eye was on them. It wasn't common to see either of them with a member of the opposite sex, and everyone was interested.

As soon as they were out of sight of the camp, Penelope dropped his arm. She didn't want him to think she was flirting with him, because she really did just want to pretend to be courting. She'd been through enough in recent months, and she didn't want to start a relationship. She just wasn't ready.

"What makes a girl who was raised on a plantation leave home and go west on the trail with no one to help her?"

Penelope didn't want to tell him the full story. It still hurt too much, so she told him the same thing she'd told Betty Bentley. "As a little girl, my mother was unable to nurse me, so one of the slaves was called in as a wet nurse. She'd had a little girl the very day I was born, and that little girl and I became the best of friends. We played and did everything together. My mother was mortified."

He smiled. "I think that sounds like a good friendship."

"It was. Muriel was the friend that kept me going. When we were ten, my father sold her to another plantation owner, separating her from her parents, just to get her away from me. I know that's why he did it, because he told me. He said that a girl of my station should never be friends with a slave's child."

"I see."

"Until that day, I'd never thought much about the fact that we owned these people who lived and worked on our land. But I couldn't get it out of my head. Every time there was a slave auction, I'd spend all night praying that Muriel would come back. Her mother cried for her every day." Penelope shook her head. "It's a barbaric practice, and I finally had enough of it. No matter how many times I begged my father to free our slaves, he refused. So, I left. My family doesn't know where I've gone."

"And if they did?" he asked.

"I really don't know. I believe my father would force me to marry so there would be no hope of me leaving again. He was already planning my alliance with a neighbor's son, but I begged for another year or two so I could be ready. When my mother agreed with me, he capitulated. We were to be married next month." And the thought of even kissing Reginald still turned her stomach as it had when she was back home. She knew she'd made the right decision.

"And how old are you?" he asked.

"I was eighteen in March."

"That's barely old enough to marry. I think a girl could marry for love at eighteen, but if it's an arranged marriage it would need to be a little later in life. Give the young lady a chance to meet someone she cares for, and then if that doesn't work out, she can tell her father what qualities she's looking for in a husband so he can search for her. But that's only my opinion, of course, and I have no children."

"Tell me about you. Where are you from?"

"I was born and raised in Independence. I've been helping people get their wagons ready to go west, but I'm ready to follow now. There are more blacksmiths than Independence can really handle at this point. I like the idea of going somewhere that I'm needed."

"I do too. But who needs a debutante for anything?" She didn't mention the dress shop she was thinking of opening when she arrived in Oregon, because that was something too new in her mind. No, she needed more time to mull over exactly how she wanted to do that.

He smiled at her. "Well, I could certainly enjoy having one in my life."

She laughed softly. "I don't know that I'm ready for that."

"I know you're not. I can see something more is bothering you than what you've told me. That's all right though. You'll tell me when you're ready if you ever are."

"Thank you for understanding." It was strange, but she was drawn to this man. A lot more than she'd been drawn to her fiancé, Reginald.

He stopped walking and turned. "We've probably gone far enough. Next time we walk, I'll need to remember my rifle. There's no telling what we could run into here."

"Indians, you mean?" She was afraid of running into a tribe of Indians. That was her biggest fear on the trail. Indians were wild and they liked to take white women as their own.

"No, not Indians. From what I understand they haven't been a big problem on the trail. No, I'm thinking about things like wild animals. Rattlesnakes and buffalo." *And white men.*

She shuddered. "You're talking to a girl who has been protected her entire life. The idea of encountering either of those is frightening for me."

"We haven't gone far from camp, and I really will remember my rifle next time. I can't believe I forgot it."

"Are you planning to settle near the others?" she asked.

"Settle near the others? What does that mean?"

"Several of the families are all planning to settle in the same area, so they can continue the friendships made on the trail. They think they'll be safer if they band together." Penelope had been invited to join the settlement, but she wasn't sure how people would feel about an unmarried woman running amok. It wasn't as if she knew how to do anything useful. Thankfully she had the pearls her mother had given her when she turned sixteen and several other pieces of jewelry she could sell to keep her going. Until she found a husband of course. For a woman it was always about finding a husband.

"I didn't know that. I think it would be nice. Especially to settle somewhere near the doctor. I like knowing there's someone around to help if I'm sick. Or if I get burned. That's always the biggest fear for a blacksmith. A bad burn."

She frowned. "Have you been burned before?"

Herb shrugged. "There's not a blacksmith who hasn't." He held up one of his hands. There were small scars covering it. "Occupational hazard. Thankfully, I've never had a *bad* burn. My father did once, and he has talked to me a dozen times about how to prevent something like that."

"I see." She didn't like the idea of him being burned. Not even a small one. She couldn't believe she was feeling protective of this man who had worked so hard to protect her.

"Thanks again for supper tonight," he said as they came within sight of camp.

"Thank you for all you've done for me. I don't know what I was thinking. I really did believe I could hitch my own team in the mornings and after the noon meal. I was very naïve." She'd tried once and failed miserably. Thankfully, he was always waiting to help.

"Well, I'm happy to be able to help. Take my arm," he said, offering it. "Let's make sure it really does look like we're courting. The men will be more likely to leave you alone that way."

"I haven't had any problem with the men in camp," she said, but she knew there always could be trouble.

"I know. Let's keep it that way." He walked her back to her camp. "Thank you for a lovely time," he said loudly, hoping others would hear.

"I enjoyed myself," she said, not realizing until that moment, it was true. She hadn't expected Herb to be able to carry on a conversation, but it had been very nice. "I will see you in the morning, and I do hope you'll join me for supper again tomorrow."

"I'd love to."

After he'd walked off, she thought about what she could cook the next evening for him. She'd watched the other women cook, and she'd learned a few things. She would make a jerky gravy and serve it with some of her potatoes and carrots. It would be a lovely meal. At least she hoped it would.

She pulled out her bedroll and climbed under the wagon where she slept many nights, thinking about what had brought her to where she was. The journey from Virginia to Independence had seemed awful at the time, but she now knew it had been easy compared to this portion of the trip. She'd at least been able to travel in a stagecoach then, and now...now she was driving a team of oxen twenty miles every day. It was a very different life than the one she'd always thought she'd live.

But she couldn't abide even another day of slavery once she'd learned of Muriel's fate. How could she?

Before she slept, she said a prayer for safe travels the next day, and another for Muriel's soul. Some believed that the slaves and all of those who came from Africa didn't have souls, but she knew better. When your life was entwined with one of the slaves, you came to understand the only differences between them and you were their circumstance and the color of their skin.

*****

Herb's prayer as he climbed into his bedroll was very different than Penelope's. He thanked God that she'd had trouble with her wagon, and he'd had to come to her rescue.

Since their time camped in Independence before their journey began, he'd had his eye on Penelope. He could tell she'd been gently bred, though her clothes were looking more and more like everyone else's as they traveled further and further.

He'd wanted to go to her and beg for her hand in marriage that evening, already knowing how he felt about her, but he knew that it wasn't the right time. No, it would be better if they got to know one another a little better before they made such a huge decision. Well, she needed to get to know him better. He already knew she was the one he wanted to be with for the rest of his days.

He prayed that their time together would make her be open to marrying him. He didn't know how it was going to come about, but it was his deepest desire, and those were things he always put before God.

*****

The following day was a typical day on the trail for Penelope. She'd imagined every day would be different and she would see many exciting things. And there were exciting things to see...on rare occasions. But most days were the same. Walking or driving along a dusty trail beside a river. Monotonous didn't begin to describe it.

As she drove, Penelope had too much time to think about things she wished she didn't. She thought about the day Muriel had been sold, and her and her friend sobbing as they embraced one last time.

She remembered the weeping Muriel's mother had done every time she looked at Penelope. The letter she'd received from her friend when they were twelve saying that she was living in the big house at her new plantation, and things were going well.

Then the letter saying that she was expecting a baby, praying no one would notice.

And the final letter, which had come from the mistress of the house where Muriel had been sold. The letter that said Muriel was a husband thief and she had been whipped to death as soon as it was discovered she was carrying.

She still carried that final letter with her at all times. It served as a reminder that people were cruel and that she didn't want any part of slavery. Ever.

Penelope's thoughts were still on Muriel as she started supper that evening. She didn't know how she would have made it through cooking if it hadn't been for the book of receipts she'd found at the general store in Independence. She'd also had some time watching people cook as she had slipped into the kitchen whenever Muriel was required to be there to help with the work. She wasn't allowed to touch anything, and had to sit watching quietly, but no one had told her parents she was doing something forbidden.

Of course, Muriel never should have learned to read, either, but Penelope had been careful to listen to everything her teacher had said so she could teach Muriel. They'd never dreamed they would be separated at such a young age, but they were prepared when it had happened.

Penelope made exactly what she'd thought about making, and when she tasted the gravy she smiled. It was actually good. There was a little more pressure on her to cook good meals with Herb sharing them with her. When she'd cooked for just herself it hadn't mattered nearly so much if the meal hadn't been perfect.

After dealing with the livestock, Herb joined her at her fire. "That smells good."

"I hope you like it. I don't have a chance to hunt, so I seem to always miss out on the fresh meat. Thankfully, Betty Bentley has become my friend, and she makes sure I get as much as she can without upsetting anyone else."

"I could hunt on Sunday if you'd like. Then we could dry the meat together."

She pursed her lips. "If I let you hunt for me, and help me dry meat, then I'll need to do your laundry in exchange."

His eyes widened. "You don't need to do my wash for me."

"If you're hunting for me, I do. I won't be a burden on anyone. Even a man as nice as you are." She handed him a tin plate with food piled high on it. She'd used more of her food reserves than she really should have, but he'd said he would share what he'd purchased for himself with her. It would all work out in the end.

"I don't want to be a burden on you," he said softly.

"You're not. You do so much for me already, that I feel like I'm still taking advantage of you. Though I do appreciate everything you work so hard to do."

"We'll talk about it," he said, not willing to give in so quickly.

She took a big bite of her food and smiled. It was the best meal she'd made all on her own, and she was rather proud of it, though she didn't say so, not wanting to seem as if she was bragging about her skills to him.

He ate his full plateful without another word, and when he finished, he smiled. "This was delicious."

"There's more," she said. "There should even be enough for our noon meal tomorrow if you care to take it with me."

"I would really enjoy that." He noticed she hadn't baked bread like most of the women did, but perhaps she hadn't had enough time. Driving all day and then cooking at night would be difficult for anyone.

"Then that's what we'll do. It's nice not to have to eat all my meals alone."

"I was eating at Margaret Prewitt's table for ten cents a week. I'd rather eat with you."

She smiled, blushing a little. "I enjoy eating with you as well."

Chapter Two

Saturday, May 29th, 1852

I cannot wait until this evening when I can take Penelope into my arms and dance with her. I have waited for this moment from the first instance when I saw her in Independence. She is obviously from a family of wealth, but from what she's told me, I do not believe she cares if I have money or not.

I don't know how she is funding her trip, but that doesn't matter to me. I'm simply glad she is here.

Now that she's agreed to a pretend courtship with me, I feel that she will be willing to dance with me. If we don't dance, our story won't be nearly as credible. I have arranged with the other men to play without me so that I can make the most of the opportunity. They do not mind.

After a long day on the trail on Saturday, they had a light supper on Saturday night, and when Penelope went to do her wash in the river with the other women, she asked Herb for his so she could do it as well.

"You can't do the wash tonight," he said. "We need to dance, so people believe that we're truly a couple."

She couldn't believe she'd already forgotten what they talked about. "Yes, you're right. I'll do it tomorrow morning before church service."

"While you do the wash, I'll try to get some meat for us."

"Thank you. I like the way we're sharing responsibilities," she said with a smile.

They walked to the open area of the camp together for the dance, and she sat down on a rock that had been used as a chair many times before their company arrived in camp. "I always enjoy the music while I do the wash. This is my first time to be a part of it."

He smiled. "It's my favorite time of the whole week. I enjoy church services a great deal as well," he added, not wanting her to think that he was an unrighteous man, "but there is something about the music that fills my soul in a way no preaching ever could."

"I'm glad. I do enjoy dancing." She frowned at him. "Don't you usually play with the others?"

Herb shrugged. "I usually play the fiddle, but the other men understand when there's courting to be done, it must take precedence." He held his hand out to her. "I don't know any fancy dances. My dancing is more just moving to the music."

"I have been taught to follow any man's lead," she said softly, wishing she'd thought to wear one of her fanciest dresses. It would have felt so much more like home if she had, and despite her need to be away, she missed home a great deal.

"Well, then we should be able to dance together well." He led her to the middle of the dance floor, and put a hand at her waist, looking into her beautiful green eyes. He'd dreamed of this moment for a long time.

As they danced, she kept her eyes on his as she'd been taught and easily followed his lead. He wasn't a practiced dancer by any means, but he could move to the beat of the music, which she enjoyed.

At the end of the dance, without thinking, she curtseyed to him, and she felt every eye in camp on her. "I guess I shouldn't have done that."

"It's all right. People don't care where you're from."

They sat out the next dance, just listening to the music and watching the others dance. Penelope was surprised when a young lady walked into the middle of the dance floor, raised her arms and began dancing alone. She moved in strange ways and everyone gave her a wide berth.

It was a good night, and Penelope was surprised by how much she enjoyed dancing with Herb. He was a good man, and she'd always liked him for that reason, but that night, she was drawn to him. Very drawn to him in a way that surprised her.

Betty came over to talk to them for a moment, her daughter at her side. "Are you enjoying the music?"

"I love it!" Penelope said. "I think you know Mr. Jensen. He's the blacksmith."

"Yes, of course. Hello, Mr. Jensen," Betty said softly. "It's nice to officially meet you. I think a lot of Penelope."

"I do too," he said, looking at the woman in question out of the corner of his eye.

"Will you be doing your wash in the morning, Penelope?" Betty asked.

"I will."

"I hope to get a chance to visit with you then." Betty winked at her friend, and Penelope understood she wanted to know all about her being there with Herb. Of course, she did. Everyone in camp was curious about them.

"I'd like that a lot." Betty wasn't the kind of friend Muriel had been, and may never be, but it was good to have someone there in camp whom she felt she could confide some things in.

As Betty walked away, heading toward Margaret Prewitt, Penelope watched her go, wishing she was more like Betty. Betty had reached out to her to try to befriend her, and she was the only person in camp who had done that so far. It was always good to have the courage to talk to strangers, and that was something Penelope was usually lacking.

Throughout the night, other people stopped by to talk to them, but mostly to talk to Herb. Men who wanted help with their wagons, or who needed new shoes for their oxen primarily. She hadn't thought about the fact that he would need to work on Sundays because they moved every other day of the week, inch by inch getting closer to the promised land of Oregon.

She didn't hold it against him though, because he did what he needed to do for the whole company. And the people who said that you couldn't work on Sundays were people who didn't take into account the fact that pastors only worked on Sundays. Did they criticize the pastor for working on the Sabbath? She wondered why no one else thought as she did about such things.

After the dance, he walked her back to her camp and helped her spread her bedroll out under the wagon. It needed to be done, and he hated that she always did everything alone, even sleeping under her wagon instead of in a tent as she should have.

He wanted to kiss her cheek goodnight, but he'd promised no kisses for show, and he didn't feel as if he could. Instead, he kissed her hand. "I will see you tomorrow, and I will hopefully have meat in my hand."

"If you have too much work to do tomorrow, don't worry about meat. I can make do with what I have on hand." It wouldn't taste as good, but it would be filling.

"I'll keep that in mind. It depends on how many people come to me in the morning," he said.

As Penelope watched him go to his own camp for the night, she wished she knew what to say to him. He was a kind man, and she was drawn to him, but she wasn't ready for more than that. Not for a good long while yet.

*****

The following morning, Herb was out trying to get some meat when a rider came up to him. "Are you part of the wagon train up ahead?"

Herb nodded. "Yes."

"Do you know if Penelope Brainerd is part of the train? Her father has paid me to find her and take her back to her fiancé in Virginia."

Herb shook his head. "Penelope Brainwhat? I don't think we have any Penelope in camp," he lied. He knew Penelope didn't want to go back, and he was determined to keep her from needing to. No matter what it took. "I'm Herb Jensen, by the way."

"Simon Bradshaw." He reached out and shook Herb's hand.

"I'll keep an ear out for anyone named Penelope if you'd like."

The man nodded. "I'll ride on to the train ahead. I think she probably went with that group." He dug his heels into his horse's sides, racing past camp.

Herb waited until the man was out of sight before heading back to camp himself. He had to find Penelope and let her know what was happening.

When he reached the river, he saw her there with the other women, doing her wash, and he called her name. She followed him, frowning. "What is it?"

"A man just rode up on a horse, not part of our company. He asked if you were part of our wagon train, saying that your father sent him to take you back to your fiancé in Virginia."

"I don't *want* to go back." She knew if her father didn't beat her for leaving, Reginald was sure to. No, she wasn't going back to Virginia no matter what it took.

Herb frowned. "I'm not sure you'll have much choice if he finds you."

Penelope looked around her as if she was trying to find a place to hide. "What can we do?"

He was thrilled that she included him in her troubles, automatically asking him to help her find a solution. "We could marry. Then he would have no authority to take you back."

She bit her lip. "Marry? I'm not ready to marry."

"I know that. I wouldn't ask anything of you...in the bedroom way, but we need to get you safe and settled before the man comes back. He's on his way to the company before ours." He hadn't intended to ask her to marry him so soon, but he prayed she'd agree. It would keep her safe, and it would mean he would get to call her his wife. He couldn't see a negative in the situation at all.

"Oh, good, but..." She took a deep breath. The solution Herb was providing was a good one. "Yes, let's marry, but I really do need time before...well, for your husbandly rights."

"I agree. I won't require anything of you until you're ready."

"And if I'm never ready?"

"Then I'll never require anything." Herb said a silent prayer that she would return his feelings soon, because he didn't want to lead a life of celibacy, but for the time being, all that mattered was marrying her and making it seem as if they had consummated the marriage. "We'll need to make sure that it looks like we've made love when the man comes back through."

She nodded. "Of course. Should we marry now or wait until after the church service." She would like a little time to mentally prepare for the wedding, but if it wasn't safe, then she would marry immediately.

"The man was on a fast horse. I think we should marry now. I don't know how far ahead of us the other company is." Herb wanted it taken care of anyway.

The two of them walked to the preacher, Jedediah Scott, immediately. "Will you marry us?" Herb asked, skipping a greeting. He quickly explained the situation, and Jedidiah agreed immediately.

Ten minutes later, they were man and wife, and Penelope felt strangely. How was she supposed to act now? When Pastor Scott invited Herb to kiss her, she wanted to hide instead, but she obediently raised her lips. It was part of being married after all.

Thankfully, Herb seemed to understand what she was feeling because he brushed a light kiss against her lips, instead of a prolonged one like she'd seen in many weddings. It was still enough to send a jolt of electricity through her body, though, and she stared at him in surprise for a moment before heading back to get the laundry taken care of.

As she walked back to the river where both of their wash was, he smiled. "I'll go see if I can get some meat now."

"Herb..."

"Yes?"

"I can't thank you enough for always watching out for me." *How did you thank a man for spending his time taking care of you when he wasn't required to? Could thanks ever be enough?*

"I always will," he replied, picking up his rifle and walking back the direction he'd come from, more determined than ever to get some meat. There was plenty of other work to be done, but a wedding feast felt like something they should do as soon as they could.

When Penelope knelt beside Betty again, her friend looked at her. "What happened?"

"My father sent a man to look for me and take me back to Virginia. Herb and I just got married to avoid me having to go back, but I feel strange about it. It won't be a real marriage," she whispered. "Please don't tell anyone that's why we married."

"I wouldn't," Betty told her. "I've discovered on this journey that there are many reasons to marry that are not all about falling in love. Marriage is so much more than that to so many people. I wasn't in love with Malcolm when we married, but now I'm very much in love with him. Sometimes it just takes a little while for your feelings to grow."

"I hope mine do," Penelope responded. "I want to make Herb as happy as he's made me."

"Don't be afraid of the marriage bed," Betty said, a blush on her face. "I know it sounds scary, and the way my mother described it made me want to hide forever, but the truth is, it's just lovely." She seemed embarrassed by her own words, but Betty was obviously determined to tell Penelope what she thought her friend needed to know.

"I...I'm not ready for that yet."

"Then you wait if he said it was fine. But the secret my sister told me is that if he kisses you and you feel all tingly or it makes your stomach turn, it means that you have feelings for him, and you should share your bed with him."

"I will think about that." The kiss Herb had given Penelope had made her feel so much more than she'd imagined, and so had the dance. Did that mean she was ready for the marriage bed? She had no idea. None.

After finishing the wash and hanging it between her wagon and Herb's, she made a quick lunch for them to share. She realized she was going to need to sort through her belongings to combine them with his, but she...well, she wasn't ready to admit to the stash of jewelry she had hidden. She had friends whose husbands had sold off their jewelry for things they wanted that their wives didn't. No, she wasn't going to put herself in a position where that could happen.

They had lunch together, and she felt shy as she mentioned combining their rigs. "Does that mean I can start walking with the other women?" she asked. She liked the idea of being able to take her place with the other females and not always having to drive.

"I suppose it does," he said with a smile. "I would try really hard for a while to wear dresses as plain as you can find. Don't let yourself stick out in any way. If it happens that you're found here, he can't drag you away, but it'll be better to avoid the situation entirely."

"That makes sense," she said softly. "Should I work on sorting our things this afternoon? Do you mind if I dig through your wagon?"

He shook his head. "I have nothing to hide. I won't be able to help you, because I have other things to do, but I did get a rabbit for our supper."

"Oh, good! Do you like rabbit stew?" She knew there was a receipt for rabbit stew in her book, and she was getting good at following the instructions exactly.

"I do. I like it a lot." With that, he got to his feet and leaned down to kiss her cheek. It was nice he was able to do that now, and then he headed off to talk to one of the men he needed to work with that afternoon as soon as church services were over. So much to do on a Sunday. Every week it was this way.

Betty came to help Penelope with her work that afternoon, and the two of them got Penelope's wagon emptied and Herb's loaded. His was slightly larger than hers, so it made sense to combine all their things into his wagon. She hid her jewelry at the bottom of his flour sack, not wanting to admit to it yet. Penelope was certain her friend saw her do it, but Betty said nothing about it, so she pretended it hadn't happened.

After church, which was held a little later than usual that day, Penelope began the process of making the rabbit stew. She was careful to follow the instructions in her receipt exactly so that it would turn out in a way she could be proud of.

She looked into her empty wagon as the food cooked, knowing it would just end up being more debris along the side of the trail, and she had to not worry about leaving her wagon behind. It had been her first home away from her parents, and her first taste of freedom, and she was loathe to leave it behind, but she knew it was the symbol of her freedom she wanted to keep and not the object itself.

When Herb came back to their fire for supper, he said, "I have one more set of oxen to reshod after supper. I'm sorry our first day as man and wife will have to be interrupted that way, but I don't really have a choice."

Penelope nodded. "I understand. You have to do your job." She wondered if he was paid for the little jobs he did along the trail, but she decided not to ask. She couldn't question his finances if she didn't want him questioning hers.

"This stew turned out very well," he said, smiling at her. "I had no idea you were such a good cook."

She smiled. "I didn't either. I bought a book of receipts in Independence, but other than that, the only cooking I've ever been party to was watching as my childhood friend learned to cook back in Virginia."

"You're doing remarkably well for a woman who has never cooked before." Her cooking certainly wasn't the best Herb had ever tasted, but she was doing an admirable job.

"Thank you." She wasn't sure if he was only being kind or if he actually meant it but either way, she was pleased. Learning to cook hadn't come naturally to her, and she worked at it every day.

While she washed dishes, he went off to shoe the last pair of oxen. He still wasn't back when she finished, so she took their clothes off the line and carefully folded them. They couldn't look perfect on the trail, but at least they would be clean. She wasn't about to iron while they were traveling this way.

When Herb arrived back, she was just putting the last of the clothes away. "Would you like to walk now that supper is over?" he asked.

"I would. I'd like that very much," she responded. She was surprised at how much she'd begun to look forward to their walks.

Together, they walked the trail where they had traveled the previous day, and she held his arm tightly the entire time. This time it was a bit harder for her to keep up appearances, because they were married, and it felt so strange to her.

When they had gone as far as he wanted, and they were about to turn around and walk back, she stepped close to him. "I'd like you to kiss me with no one watching please." She needed to know if the tingles happened as Betty had said they would. She wasn't sure if it was just something that had happened during the wedding, or if it would be normal for her.

When Herb took her into his arms and slowly lowered his mouth to hers, she held her breath, waiting to see what would happen. His lips touched hers, and she felt it again. The butterflies in her stomach and the tingles rushing through her body. He made her feel things she'd never felt before, and she loved feeling them. She wanted to always feel them.

Her arms wrapped around him and she moved closer to him, tilting her head to one side. Herb simply gathered her to him and continued kissing her.

Finally, she broke off the kiss, staring up at him with surprise. "That was...amazing."

He smiled. "I always knew when I got the chance to kiss you, it would be that way. Special for both of us." He was pleased she'd found it pleasing as well.

"It was special for you too?" she asked.

He nodded. "I've never courted anyone seriously, so it was really my first kiss too." He stroked her cheek. "Thank you for sharing it with me."

"What are we going to do if that man comes back?" she asked, not able to keep her mind focused on him now that the kiss was over. The man was constantly hanging over her head, dangling there like a machete about to fall and kill her.

"He *will* come back, Penelope. And what we'll do is tell him we're married, and he can't have you. I'll make sure the other men in camp know that he will be coming around, and together we'll make a plan. Just make sure you don't go off alone."

"I'll do my best."

He frowned. "If you have to walk without a man near you, then make sure Mary is there. Mary always has that musket of hers, and I can be certain she can protect you if I'm not there to do it."

"Would you teach me to shoot?" she asked. "I would like to be able to take care of myself if at all possible."

"I will start that tomorrow evening. The light is getting too dim now."

"I'll stay close to Mary tomorrow." Penelope didn't know Mary well, and she certainly wasn't a close friend of hers, but she would stay with her. She would do anything to avoid going back to Virginia and having to marry Reginald.

As they walked toward camp, she stayed close to him, clinging to his arm. Her eyes watched in every direction as she worried that the man her father had sent was behind every bush. There, ready to grab her and drag her back to Virginia, kicking and screaming if necessary.

When they got back to camp, Herb put up her tent. "I don't need a tent," she told him.

"*We* need a tent though," he said loudly. "It's the only way we'll have privacy for our wedding night."

She blushed as she realized that he had just announced to the entire camp that he planned to consummate their marriage that night. She knew he wouldn't, but it was best if everyone thought they were. Of course, it made sense that he had said it so loudly, whether she liked it or not.

Once the tent was erected, she climbed into it, spreading out her bedroll. He put his in with hers and set it as far from hers as possible. "I know I promised you not to make love yet, and I plan to keep that promise, but it has to look like something is happening between us."

"Yes, I understand," she said. She lay atop her bedroll, staring up at the tent. It was odd to be in this position, and it certainly wasn't how God wanted them to be. No, he intended for men and women sleeping together to be intimate. There was no doubt about it.

He reached over and touched her hand. "Goodnight, Penelope."

"Goodnight, Herb." And that was that. Their wedding night had been successfully accomplished, and now they could continue on with their marriage. It would be easy from here. It had to be.

As Penelope lay there, she closed her eyes and thanked God for the fact that Herbert had been the one to intercept the man her father had sent. No one else would have known to say she wasn't there. Or to send the man on. No one else would have married her immediately to save her from having to go back to Virginia.

Beside her, Herb thanked God for the opportunity to make Penelope his wife so much sooner than he thought he'd be able to. Life was going to be different now that they were together. Her problem had become his perfect time to convince her that she needed to be his wife for more reasons than just trying to escape a fiancé she cared nothing for. He loved her, and he prayed he'd be able to get her to love him back.

Chapter Three

Monday, June first, 1852

I find myself married to a virtual stranger, and I'm not sure how to feel about it. When a man came to camp looking for me, I did what I felt I needed to do, but I'm very fearful of what he'll do when he comes back through. I'm thankful to be married to Herb, who is making a plan with the other men to protect me when Mr. Bradford comes back through, but I pray the plan will be unnecessary.

I will do whatever I have to do to hide from the danger that is coming for me. I must. I cannot go back to Virginia and the life I left there. I cannot.

Penelope went in search of Mary Hastings as soon as the wagons pulled out the following morning. "Herb asked me to make sure I'm always with you, and you have your musket with you," she said quietly.

Mary frowned. "Herb is the blacksmith?"

Penelope nodded, realizing she hadn't known the man's name until a couple of days ago, and she shouldn't expect others to know it just because she did. "There's a man who is looking for me. He was told I'm not part of this company yesterday, but I'm almost certain he'll be back. His name is Simon Bradford, and he wants to take me back to someone who will hurt me."

"Are you in trouble with the law?" Mary asked, looking skeptical.

"Not at all. My father isn't pleased that I left our home instead of marrying the man he chose for me. I just couldn't stay there and be part of that culture for another minute." Penelope said a silent prayer that Mary would agree to be her protector during the day.

"I see. Yes, I'll keep my musket with me and spend all my time with you when Mr. Jensen can't."

"Thank you."

"In return, if you see an animal let me know. I want fresh meat for supper tonight." Mary had always seemed very single-minded to Penelope. She wanted to hunt and that's what she did.

Penelope smiled. "And if there's enough fresh meat, you'll share?"

Mary laughed. "Of course, I will. I love to share."

As they walked and talked, Penelope was surprised by how much like herself Mary was in some ways. And how very different they were in others. "Sounds like you married quickly, as most have on the trail. Do you like your new husband?"

Penelope choked. "Of course, I like him." Who would ask such a thing?

Mary shook her head. "There's no of course about it. I love Bob with everything inside me, but today, I don't like him very much."

"You don't?"

"No, I don't. He said the eggs I made for breakfast had shells in them, and I know they didn't, so I'm going to be mad at him for a while." Mary said the words as if they were a pronouncement, and she didn't care who felt differently about it than she did.

"You're just choosing to be angry?" Penelope thought that was quite odd.

"Sure. I'll be angry until mid-morning, and by the time we stop for our noon meal, I'll like him again. It's a good system when he's driving all day." Mary shrugged, and Penelope took that to mean it was something the other woman did often.

"I see." Penelope really didn't know what to think of that, so she changed the subject by asking about where Mary had grown up, and then Mary took over the entire conversation. It was easy enough to get her to stop talking about her choice to be angry with Bob.

When they stopped for the noon meal, Mary stayed with Penelope until Herb was there with them, and Herb nodded his thanks to Mary. "Thank you for watching over her the way you have. I hope you know I really appreciate it."

"I'm happy to do it," Mary said as she hurried off to eat with Bob.

"What's for lunch?" Herb asked.

"I have a feeling you're going to be asking me that a lot in the days to come." Penelope liked that he was dependent on her for his meals, just as she was dependent upon him for protection.

"Of course, I will. It's my job." He grinned at her as she pulled out what was left of the rabbit stew from the evening before. She scooped up two bowls of the concoction and handed him one of them. He licked his lips in anticipation. "This is going to be just as good the second time around," he said, taking the spoon she gave him and eating it happily. "Rabbit stew was my favorite meal when I was a boy. My mother never made it, but every time I went to a friend's house, his mother served it."

"I don't think I'd ever had it before last night."

He gaped at her for a moment before nodding. "I forget how privileged your background was."

"Everything I ever had was built on the backs of men and women from Africa. Our family owned over a hundred slaves. There were ten working in the house and countless more in the fields." She shook her head, thinking of the suffering her life of luxury had brought to so many others.

"Your house must have been enormous."

"There were eight bedrooms," she told him. "I had a teacher who was there to teach only me."

"Did you have no brothers and sisters?"

"A younger brother. My father always wanted to make a good match for me, so he could leave the plantation to someone he trusted until my brother came along. I think that's one of the reasons I want to go west. I think I should be able to own property whether I'm a man or a woman, and out west it doesn't matter so much."

"That's a really good point," he said. "I agree that women should be able to own property and to not be beholden to men for everything they have. I'm just glad we both chose the same wagon train to go west."

"So am I," she said, smiling shyly. "I certainly didn't expect to marry before we were halfway there."

"I didn't either, but I can't say that I'm disappointed things turned out this way. I'm married to the prettiest woman west of the Mississippi. No other man can say that."

She laughed. "I don't think you can say it either. I'm not pretty. I'm just...well, I'm me." She'd always been told she was pretty by her parents, but she could hear Muriel's mother's voice in her ear. "Pretty is as pretty does. You be nice to people, and you'll be the prettiest girl in all Virginia." She hated being called pretty now. It was what was on the inside of her that mattered.

"Well, I'd have to fight anyone who tried to say it," he said.

"You're not going to fight with someone just because they think someone else is prettier than me. That would be ridiculous."

"I suppose it might, but I'd do it anyway, because I don't like it when other men lie to me, and there's no one around half as pretty as you."

She shook her head. "Maybe I should wash our dishes."

He chuckled. "Afraid you're going to lose this argument?"

"Not at all. I know I will. So, I'm not going to keep talking about it."

She gathered their dishes and the empty pot the stew had been in and added cold river water to the hot water she'd had boiling since before they started the meal. "I told Mary what she needed to know about the danger to me. I hope you don't mind that."

"I don't at all. I'm just glad someone else will be watching your back when I can't be with you. I do need to take the time to drive all day."

"I know you do. I'll feel safer since I'll have the time with Mary." Penelope shrugged. "She can be odd at times, but I really think I like her."

"And I like you," Herb said, grinning at her. "Let me wipe the dishes while you wash them."

"That's women's work!" she protested.

"And you've been doing men's work since we left Independence. It doesn't hurt me one bit," he said.

"Just like the men's work has never hurt me."

"No, it hasn't."

Penelope was glad he wasn't a man who minded helping with women's chores. It would make things much easier for them in the future. She stored their lunch dishes into the back of the wagon as soon as they were dry, knowing they'd have to head out again soon.

When they parted ways to begin their afternoon journey, Herb waited until Mary was there to watch over Penelope. He realized he was probably being overly cautious, but he found he didn't care.

"Thank you," he said to Mary as he headed to the wagon.

They were halfway through their afternoon drive when the wagon in the front of the line stopped, causing all of the others to stop as well. Mr. Bradford was going down the line of wagons, showing each driver something.

When he got to Herb, he was shown a sketch of Penelope. He shrugged as if he didn't know anything and then the man moved on. He'd briefed all the other drivers that morning about how there was someone looking for his wife, and they all agreed to try to conceal her identity as best they could. He wanted to jump down and go and protect his wife, but it would be telling. He just had to pray that everyone did as they'd said they would.

When the wagons started rolling again, he worried until Penelope came up to walk beside him. "Mary realized what was happening, and she hid me in the pastor and Hannah's wagon." She'd known he'd need to see her to believe she was all right, so she'd made sure to go to him as soon as she could.

"Oh good. Everyone denied knowing you?"

"Yes. Thank you for letting everyone know to hide me."

"They're not taking you back as long as I'm alive."

"I'm grateful." Though she knew if it came to it, she wouldn't let Herb risk his life for her. He was too precious to be thrown away like the trash that littered the trail.

He frowned at that, not wanting her gratitude. "You're my wife. It's my job to protect you."

"I know," she said softly, returning to her spot beside Mary.

When they stopped that evening, there was fresh venison that Mary had gotten with her musket, and Penelope decided to make a roast from it. She put the roast into her pot, added some carrots and some rice, and then she added water. Mary had given her advice on how to make the meat into a tasty meal, so she covered it and put it right into the fire.

It was something she'd never cooked, not having known enough people to share in the meat before that day. She was happy to be able to make a good meal for Herb though.

She had started some bread rising while they were on their noon meal, and she tucked that into the fire as well.

When Herb finished with the livestock, he stopped by the fire. "I need to change some shoes on a pair of oxen. Will supper hold?"

It was nowhere near ready yet, so Penelope nodded and sent him on his way. Mary had set up camp right beside her, and Penelope and Herb both knew she was safe, so they didn't worry about him being gone for a short while.

By the time he returned, she had supper ready, and she fixed their plates. "How was your first day walking?" he asked.

"It was good. I'm a little sore from it, but I expect that to be a constant thing until we reach Oregon."

"It probably will be," he said. "I hope you enjoyed your time with the other women."

"I did. I walked with Mary, Hannah, Margaret, and Betty. The only one of them I really knew before today was Betty." She frowned. "I feel like I should make an effort to get to know Trudie. She and I were the only women on this trip alone, and I don't think I realized just how lonely I was until today, when I had companions again. I think she needs a friend."

"Then you should be that friend," he said. "You can do that."

"I'm going to try. Do you mind if I invite her to share our supper tomorrow evening?" she asked.

"Not at all. You might also want to invite the widow we found on the side of the trail and her family. I cannot remember her name, but it would be nice for her to join us."

"I'd like that a lot," she said, nodding. I'll make sure to ask her to join us tomorrow night. Or ask Trudie tomorrow and ask the widow on Wednesday."

"Either way. I think we'll both be happy to have some company at meals and to make new friends."

"Do you have trouble making friends?" she asked, a little surprised.

"Sometimes," he said. "I'm a quiet man by nature, and I don't like to talk about religion, politics, or the weather, which seem to be the only things men ever want to talk about."

"You should join the women then. We talk about quilting, and food, and doing the wash." Penelope grinned at him.

"I think I'll forgo that stimulating conversation and spend my time alone, thank you very much."

Penelope laughed. "I guess we could just talk to each other, but we might get bored with that as well."

"We might, but I don't think we will. We're good at talking to one another." He smiled, reaching out and stroking her cheek in a gesture that was starting to feel familiar to her.

"You're a good man, Herb. I like that about you."

"I like everything about you," he said, not even joking a little bit. She was a wonderful woman. "Do you want to walk after dishes? Or are you too tired from walking all day?"

She shrugged. "I wouldn't mind a leisurely walk, but if I start whimpering, it's time to turn around and come back to camp."

"That sounds reasonable to me. I'll try not to do anything to make you whimper."

"Good. I hate acting like a small child."

"We all do, but sometimes it helps to whimper. I don't know why, but it does. And then you have to just put your chin up and deal with the pain."

"That makes a lot of sense to me," she said. "I'll do my best to keep my chin up all the time."

"I hope you will."

During their walk, they walked up the river in the direction they hadn't gone yet, and he had his rifle at his side. "You usually want to walk the other way," she said.

"That's the way the man looking for you went."

"Do you think he'll be back?" she asked, frowning. "I assumed the danger was over."

"I do think he'll be back. He's not giving up. He had a portrait of you that I wanted to steal from him so *I* would have a portrait of you. But he showed all the drivers." Herb shook his head, feeling like the situation was more dire than ever.

She bit her lip. "Maybe I should leave so I'm not putting anyone else in danger."

"We're in the middle of the Oregon Trail. You are not going to go anywhere that I don't go with you."

"All right." She didn't want to go anywhere, and it wasn't just that she was worried about the man looking for her. She didn't want to leave her new husband. She didn't know where that thought was coming from, but it was definitely there.

He put his arm around her waist, and she rested her head on his shoulder. "It feels like letting you touch me is still doing something wrong."

He laughed. "It's not. We're married now."

"I know. I just...well, I have very strict etiquette in my head, and I feel like I'm doing something wrong when I don't follow whatever it says."

"Nowhere does it say you can't touch the man you married, does it?" Herb asked.

"No, but we haven't been married long enough that it feels like I should let you touch me."

"Do you want me to wait ten years before I put my arm around you?" he asked, a grin on his face.

"No, I think we're good." She smiled up at him for a moment. "Thank you for doing so much to keep me safe."

"I'm happy to do whatever you need," he said.

Penelope stopped walking. "I feel like this is the only place we can kiss. Out here on the prairie when no one can see us."

"I'm happy to kiss you whenever you want wherever you want. Kissing you is one of my favorite things, actually."

"Then kiss me now."

This time Herb wasn't as tentative with his touch. He stroked his hands up and down her arms as he molded his mouth to hers, parting her lips for the first time, and meeting her tongue with his own.

She gasped with surprised. "I don't think you're supposed to do that."

"We're married. I can kiss you however I want." To prove the truth in his words, he kissed her again, much more deeply this time. Her arms went around his neck and she clung to him.

When he finally broke off the kiss, they were both out of breath. "We need to stop that, or I'm going to lay you down in the grass and do something I've promised not to do until you're ready."

Her eyes widened. "I wasn't trying to give you permission to do that!"

He sighed, resting his forehead against hers. "I know you weren't. You were just enjoying the kiss, and that's okay. Just know that too many kisses like that, and I'm going to want a lot more from you."

"I see," she said, taking a deep breath. "Perhaps in a week or two, when we feel the danger has passed, I'll feel more comfortable about that."

"I sure hope so," he said. "There's nothing I want more than to make love to you at this very moment."

Penelope bit her lip. "I owe you so much. I will let you have your wedding night tonight if you need it so badly."

He shook his head. "When we finally have a wedding night, you will need it as badly as I do. I promise you this."

"Are you certain? I feel badly making you wait when you gave up your freedom just to help me." Penelope wasn't sure why he was so kind to her, but she certainly couldn't complain about it.

"It wasn't just to help you, Penelope. I gave up my freedom because I wanted to spend the rest of my life with you. There's no other reason."

She looked at him in surprise. "But...you asked me to marry you because that man was looking for me."

"Yes, I did. I would have waited for you to get to know me a little better before I asked if he hadn't come around, but I still would have asked." He stopped walking and looked into her eyes. "I've been watching you since before we left Independence. I knew the first moment I saw you that I wanted to spend my life with you."

"You did?" She didn't even remember when she'd first seen him. Why hadn't she noticed him? Even as she thought about why, she knew the answer. It was because he was a quiet man who didn't attract attention. It was one of her favorite things about him.

When they got back to camp, they erected their tent and bedded down for the night. As soon as they were in their respective bedrolls, she reached out to him. "Are you certain you don't want to..."

"I'm certain I *do* want to, but I'm also certain it will be better for you if we wait, so that's what we're going to do. You're a special woman, Penelope, and I don't want to rush you."

"Thank you, Herb." She rolled toward him and pressed her lips to his cheek. "You're the best man I could have asked for. I see that now."

"I'm glad you think so." And he hoped she was telling the truth about only waiting a week or so. He wasn't sure how much longer he'd be able to wait. He really had no idea how difficult it would be to lie next to this woman every night and not make love to her the way he wanted.

As soon as she closed her eyes, Penelope thanked God for him. And she thanked Him for the entire wagon train being willing to pretend they had never seen her. She hadn't obeyed her father by leaving, but God had sent her Herb anyway. A man who was taking care of her. She didn't know what she could have possibly done to deserve a man like him, but whatever it was, she was glad she'd done it.

When she closed her eyes to sleep, she realized it was the first night she'd forgotten to pray for Muriel's soul, so she added that to her prayer as well, wishing her friend was there with her.

But she knew, deep down, that if her friend had still been there, she never would have left on the trail or married. And she would still not see a problem with slavery.

Chapter Four

Tuesday, June 2nd, 1852

I have taken the lovely Penelope Brainerd as my bride. I will not explain the circumstances now except to say I must now find a way to protect her from a past she is trying to escape from.

We continue along the north branch of the Platte River for a few more days, praying that no rain comes before we find the right place to cross. This is one of the most dangerous crossings of our entire journey.

Before they started out on Tuesday morning, Penelope found Trudie to ask her to join them for supper that night. "We were the only two women on this journey alone, and now it's only you. I feel like that should be sufficient for us to become friends," Penelope explained.

"I'm not so sure," Trudie said. "I don't need any friends."

"Sure, you do. Everyone needs companionship. Tell me what has you so frightened."

Trudie looked over her shoulder and all around, as if she was hiding something, but Penelope couldn't get her to budge on what it was. "Please just come eat with us. It'll save you from having to cook tonight, and I'm sure you're tired of cooking for one."

"Of course, I'm tired of cooking for one." Trudie kicked at a rock on the ground. "All right, I'll come to supper, but you're not to ask me any questions."

"I won't ask anything other than how your day was."

"I won't tell you where I'm from or why I'm going to Oregon," Trudie warned.

"Then I'll be certain not to ask those questions in particular." Penelope had no idea what the other woman's problem was, but she was willing to befriend her anyway. She truly felt badly for the prickly woman.

As they walked that day, she asked Mary to try to find her another bit of meat for her pot that night. "I'm having my first guest as a married woman, and since I can't serve a meal on china, I feel like I should at least serve some meat."

Mary laughed softly. "I'll see what I can do. I like to be the provider of meat for many people, so let's see if we can spot a buffalo today." Mary had told Penelope that she was sad she hadn't been the first to bring in a buffalo from their wagon train, and Penelope knew her friend meant it. The girl loved to hunt more than anything, it seemed.

By noon, they had a buffalo, and they hung it from the back of the wagon Mary shared with Bob. "We'll need to strip it at lunch time and distribute the meat," Mary said. "It's going to break the wagon otherwise. It's just too heavy to do it this way."

Penelope nodded. "I'm happy to do that. I will help in any way I can."

"Have you ever helped carve up a buffalo into roasts?" Mary asked, looking at Penelope who she obviously thought was too frail for many of the things they were doing.

"I haven't, but I will." It wasn't something she'd ever done, but only because she'd never had the opportunity. She didn't think it would bother her too terribly much, and if it did, she'd get over it.

Mary smiled. "I knew you were made of stronger stuff than you look like you are."

"I certainly hope I am," Penelope said. She knew she looked like she needed someone to take care of her, but she felt like she'd done a good job so far in doing all that she possibly could.

After their noon meal, while most of the camp napped around them, Penelope, Herb, Bob, and Mary carved up the buffalo, portioning it out for different families. Penelope and Herb took a larger chunk than they usually would, because they were sharing their supper with Trudie. Mary took some for her mother's family, some for Hannah and Jedediah, some for Betty and Malcolm, and some for Margaret and Jamie and their girls. Penelope asked for some she could give the widow, Mrs. Gabriel, and Mary made sure she cut off a nice large slab for the family that the previous wagon train had left behind.

After that, they offered it to many of the other travelers, because they didn't want to have to dry it that day. No, it would be good for everyone to have fresh meat anyway.

As they parted ways, leaving the bones on the side of the road to be found by the next company to come through, Herb grinned at Penelope. "Nice friend you have there!"

"I know. She's better with her musket than most men are." She smiled at him. "I'll take this to Mrs. Gabriel after putting ours in the back of the wagon. I can't wait to cook tonight." Penelope had found she took great pleasure in cooking when the ingredients were plentiful as they were that night, and she was already planning what she would cook for supper with their guest.

She took the second roast to the widow, who accepted it gratefully. "I can't pay for this."

"No one would ever ask you to," Penelope said with a smile. She liked what she knew of the other woman, and she was so happy that she could help in some small way.

"Thank you."

"You're very welcome. I was wondering also if you and your family would like to have supper with my husband and I tomorrow evening. I'm not sure yet what I'll make, but whatever it is, I would like you to share it with us."

The widow nodded, looking excited, which wasn't an emotion Penelope had ever seen on her face. "We would be pleased to join you. May I make a bread and dessert?"

Penelope nodded. "That would be wonderful Thank you for the offer."

As she hurried back to camp, she was glad she'd reached out to the woman. She had four children, and she was fighting hard to keep going after her husband's recent death.

By the time Penelope returned to their wagon, Herb was hitching up the team. "That was one noon break that was over too quickly," she said. Usually there was time to rest before they started their afternoon travels, but with the carving of the buffalo, there was no time at all.

Herb nodded, finishing his task and then kissing her cheek. "I look forward to some time alone with you this evening, wife."

"And I look forward to time alone with you," she said, falling into line with the other women as the wagons lined up to drive away.

Mary was very animated that afternoon, talking to everyone about something that had happened back in Independence, and making them all laugh. That was one of the best things about Mary in Penelope's opinion. She was fun to talk to, and she told the best stories.

Penelope found herself walking beside Hannah, the pastor's wife that afternoon, and Penelope found she was very intimidated by the other woman. It was odd to be with her, because she didn't seem to be one of those holier than thou preacher's wives. No, she was more like all the other women. It was refreshing to see how sweet she was.

"Is it hard being married to a pastor?" Penelope asked.

"No harder than being married to a blacksmith, I'm sure," Hannah grinned. "I love Jed, and I'd love him if he was a grave digger. He's a very good man."

"I've noticed that about him. My Herb surprises me with what a wonderful man he is. I barely knew him when we married, but I find myself feeling closer to him every day." Penelope realized she had been truly blessed with a man like Herb. He cared for her a great deal.

"Jed says he's a good man, and I believe him. He does a lot of work on the trail for people, and he never expects even a dime in payment. He keeps saying that all of us arriving in Oregon together will be his payment."

Penelope smiled at that. "We've talked about settling close to the rest of you, and I hope it goes well."

"I'm sure it will. We have ranchers, farmers, a pastor, a doctor, and now a blacksmith. I think we're all going to be very happy in a little community together. We just have to find the right place." Hannah seemed excited at the prospect of finding just the right place.

"I'm sure that won't be too difficult."

"I hope not. Everyone is happy we don't have to say goodbye to each other at the end of the trail. There are a few I wouldn't mind saying it to, but then I remember I'm a Christian, and I love my neighbors."

Penelope laughed. "I didn't know preacher's wives were allowed to think like the rest of us."

"Apparently we are, because God has not yet struck me with lightning."

"He's a *good* God."

"There you go again, Hannah, talking religion," Margaret said with a wink at Penelope.

Hannah shrugged. "Its my lot in life."

"You did marry a preacher," Betty said with a smile.

"And you married the doctor. What does that say about our intelligence?" Hannah asked.

"I don't know what it says for yours, but I hope for me it means I won't have sick children." Betty looked toward her new daughter who was playing with Margaret's children, obviously making sure she was safe.

They all laughed. "I'm having supper with Trudie tonight," Penelope said, wondering how the others would feel.

Betty wrinkled her nose. "She's not terribly pleasant, but I hope you have a nicer time with her than I did."

"I will try," Penelope said, wondering what it was about Trudie that she wanted to keep people at arm's length. Penelope was truly just trying to be a friend, and Trudie had already slapped away her hand many times.

Penelope started cooking immediately after they arrived at their campsite for the night, and she turned the meat she'd been given into a roast with potatoes and carrots, and she made a gravy for it all. She didn't have time to bake a loaf of bread, but she was sure there was enough other food that they'd be all right anyway.

By the time Herb came to join her, Trudie was heading their direction. Penelope smiled wide. "How was your day?"

Trudie shrugged. "I drove all day like I do every day."

"Are you looking forward to actually finding the elephant?" Penelope asked, referring to their arrival in Oregon.

"In some ways I am," Trudie said. "I like the idea of having my own parcel of land that no one can take away from me. That's what I'm really excited about."

"I'm sure that will happen for you very soon," Penelope said. "I didn't plan to share my parcel with anyone either, but Herb came along, and I have to now." She winked at her husband to let him know she was only joking.

"I won't be marrying ever," Trudie said, her eyes looking haunted, but Penelope knew better than to ask what had happened to her.

"I said that once too." Penelope shrugged. "I do hope you find happiness in whatever form it presents itself." With that, she served the plates handing one to Trudie first. "I'm so glad you're joining us for supper tonight."

"Me too," Trudie said. "I think I could get used to you."

Penelope noticed the other woman hadn't said she could be her friend. Just that she could get used to her. She'd have to take it for what it was.

Herb looked annoyed, but Penelope shook her head. She hoped he knew that meant that she didn't think he should say anything about the way Trudie was acting. For Trudie, her demeanor was sunshine and flowers compared to how it usually was.

While they ate, Penelope steered the conversation toward subjects that wouldn't upset the other woman. "I hope it's not as hot in Oregon as it is here," she said. "From what I've read, the temperature is supposed to be mild."

"That's what I've read as well," Herb said, following her lead.

"I enjoyed walking with Hannah and the other ladies today," Penelope said. "Hannah is different than any preacher's wife I've ever met. In a good way, of course."

"No two people are the same, and you really can't treat them as if they are," Trudie said. "Someone may do something that seems deplorable, but when you understand their reasons for it, it's not as bad as it seemed."

"Can you give us an example of what you mean?" Herb asked.

Trudie shrugged. "What if someone stole a loaf of bread. The act is deplorable. But then you find out he has six children to feed, his wife died, and he has no way to earn money. His motives are good while his actions are wrong. You have to look at each person and judge their motives before you decide they're terrible people."

"That's really true," Penelope said. She was surprised the other woman had such deep thoughts about anything with her unfortunate behavior. Perhaps she was explaining in her own way that no one should judge her actions. Only her motives.

After supper, Trudie left, not offering to wash the dishes, but Penelope hadn't expected her help. She knew the other woman well enough to know that it wouldn't be part of the evening, and it didn't bother her.

As soon as the dishes were done, she covered her yawn with her hand. "I think I'm going to have to forgo our walk this evening."

Herb frowned. "Aren't you sleeping well?"

"Would you be if you knew that someone was trying to force you to go somewhere you don't want to be?" Penelope just wished she could get Simon Bradford and the fact he was looking for her out of her mind.

Herb frowned. "I'm not letting him take you anywhere."

"I know you're not." Penelope wasn't truly convinced though. It was still possible she could be found and forced to go back. It wouldn't be her preference, but it could certainly happen. And then where would she be?

She'd once heard Reginald talk about how you should treat a wife like she was one of your slaves. If she didn't do as she was told, she needed to be whipped to within an inch of her life. She knew that Herb would never think or say anything like it, and she thanked God for his kindness.

There was no way she was going to be Reginald's wife, and there was no one who could force her to do so.

When she prayed that night, she thanked God for saving her from the men trying to hurt her. And she prayed for Muriel's soul. Because Muriel needed her prayers more than anyone else she knew.

Beside her, Herb reached out to her and pulled her against him, holding her. "I wish I could ease your worries."

"You can't. No one can." She sighed and nestled her head against his shoulder. "I'll be all right. I just need to get used to the idea that I could be taken at any time. But don't worry about me. If I'm taken, I'll just find a way to escape. Again and again. I won't stay with him or anyone else who owns slaves. I'm my own person, and I don't think anyone can forget it."

Once she had spoken her intention aloud, she was able to sleep, and thankfully, Herb understood.

Chapter Five

Wednesday June 3rd, 1852

Though my life has really taken a turn and things are very different than they were a week ago, I think it's good. I really enjoy spending time with Herb and getting to know him better, and it's nice to be with the other women and not have to drive all day any longer. My shoulders no longer ache like they did for a while, but the ache has taken up residence in my legs and feet instead.

I enjoyed having Trudie over for supper last night, and when I knew what subjects to shy away from, the experience was truly enjoyable. I know Trudie is hiding something, but so am I. We all are, so it doesn't matter much what she's hiding as far as I'm concerned. Oregon is for starting new lives, and she has a right to her secrets just as I have a right to mine.

Penelope made sure that Mrs. Gabriel, the widow who had been found on the side of the road, was with them as they walked the next day. She wanted to get to know the other woman so Mrs. Gabriel would feel as if she was a part of things, the same way Penelope now felt like she was part of the company. "Who drives your wagon?" she asked.

"My oldest son. He does a good job, and then I can mind the little ones." Mrs. Gabriel nodded to the small child walking beside them on the trail. "Stanley has been my rock since my husband fell ill. I'm really not sure what I would have done without him."

"I can understand that. I'm very much looking forward to our supper tonight," Penelope said.

"I am too. Thank you for inviting us. We haven't really had the opportunity to spend much time with others without feeling burdensome."

Penelope put her arm around the other woman's shoulders. "You're not a burden at all. You are a wonderful woman, and I'm so happy to have the pleasure of getting to know you."

"Thank you, Mrs. Jensen. I'm feeling rather pleased to get to know you as well."

"Please, call me Penelope."

"Only if you'll call me Katie."

"Katie it is." Penelope was ever aware of Mary right behind her with her musket, but she enjoyed her time getting to know Katie well.

Just before lunch, there was a gunshot from behind her, and though Penelope jumped, she knew it meant fresh meat for at least Mary and Bob, and hopefully for many others on the trip.

Mary laughed and shouted excitedly, and Penelope turned around to see her struggling with a doe she'd shot. Penelope immediately went to help, and the two of them worked to get the deer hoisted onto the back of Bob's wagon yet again. Penelope was thankful the wagons moved so slowly as they plodded along the prairie.

As soon as they finished their noon meal, the two couples—Bob and Mary and Herb and Penelope—spent their rest time carving up the animal and distributing meat. Penelope hadn't asked for meat that day, but she found that she was very glad to have it on another day with company coming for supper. It would help stretch her food as far as it could go.

For supper, Penelope cooked the deer meat into a stew that she hoped would be enough for the group she was feeding. Knowing that Katie had a teenage boy, she was a little worried, but she really hoped they'd still have enough for lunch the following day.

When the other family arrived, she was happy to meet all four of Katie's children and share food with them. True to her word, Katie brought a loaf of bread and a cake she'd made after they'd stopped for the evening.

"That smells delicious," Katie said. "Your mother must have been a good cook."

Penelope laughed. "I don't think my mother has ever cooked anything in her life. We had slaves for that." She wasn't sure if she'd been able to conceal her bitterness when she'd mentioned the slaves.

"Sounds like you were brought up in a different way than most of us," Katie said with a smile. She put her arm around her oldest son. "This is Stanley. He drives for us."

"It's nice to meet you, Stanley," Penelope said with a smile. "I hope you're hungry, because I made a lot."

"Ma says I have hollow legs," Stanley said, grinning at her.

"I think most boys your age do." Penelope served the stew, and everyone took a bowl. She sat on a rock beside Herb and watched as everyone else chose other places to sit. The four children sat on the ground and Katie took another rock close to the fire. "It's chilly this evening."

Katie nodded. "I think we have a storm coming in."

"We probably do," Herb said looking around. "I think it's going to be a big one too."

"I guess we're sleeping under the wagon tonight." Stanley wrinkled his nose, and Penelope was sure he liked sleeping out under the stars.

"Or in the wagon," Katie said.

"We won't all fit," Stanley said with a sigh. "I guess you're all in the wagon and as the man of the family, I'll be under it."

Katie smiled at him. "I guess you're right."

Penelope hadn't realized how much Stanley had taken on since his father's death. The boy couldn't be more than fourteen, yet he was the one driving every day and he offered to sleep out in the rain. "You're a good man, Stanley."

Stanley obviously noticed her change from calling him a boy to a man because he preened. "It's my responsibility."

"I'll go over with you after supper and see if we can make your wagon cover a little tighter to avoid getting water in there before the storm comes," Herb said, wanting to be there to help if he could.

"Thank you, Mr. Jensen," Stanley said.

While they were off taking care of the wagon, Katie helped Penelope with the dishes while the children went to find their friends to play. Only the youngest stayed there, but Penelope had found out that he was always with his mother. He obviously didn't like to be away from her, and who could blame him? He'd just lost his father recently. He might worry his mother would disappear soon too.

After the men finished, Stanley rounded up his siblings, and they ate the cake Katie had baked for dessert. "This is delicious!" Penelope said. "I wish I could make something that tastes this good. I'm just learning to cook, and I feel like I'm very inept."

"You did a wonderful job with supper," Katie said with a smile. "This is my mother's cake, and I've been making it since I was a little girl. Would you like the receipt?"

"I would love it!" Penelope saw that Herb was already on his second piece. She'd love to be able to bake something he enjoyed that much for him.

After the Gabriels had left, Herb looked at Penelope. "Would you like to walk with me?"

She smiled. Their walks had become precious to her. "I would love to. Let me just wash up the knife I used to cut the cake, and I'll be ready." Since the water was still there from the supper dishes, it only took a moment.

As they walked, she talked about Katie and how much she liked the other woman. "She's sad, and you can see it at times on her face, but she's definitely being strong for her children. Did you know her husband died of a putrid foot and not from Cholera?"

"I didn't, but I'm not surprised," he said softly. "It's a tough journey for anyone, whether they get cholera or not." He almost thought those who died quickly from the disease had it easier than those who lingered with it. He knew the journey was going to be a tough one, but he'd had no idea just how hard until they'd started out.

When they were out of sight of the camp, Penelope turned to Herb and initiated their kiss. This was what she loved so much about their walks. They could kiss and show one another physical affection without anyone watching.

Herb pulled her to him and his hands roamed over her body, touching her in places that she wasn't certain he had the right to touch, but he was her husband, so she didn't feel like she should stop him either. It was certainly a dilemma.

His touch sent little fires through her body, starting at wherever his hand was and shooting straight to her core. "I think I'm ready," she said when he pulled away. Granting him his husbandly rights no longer felt like something to be feared.

"Ready for what?" he asked. Surely, she didn't mean what he wanted her to mean.

"I think I'm ready to make love with you, Herb."

He gaped at her for a moment, surprised. "I thought we were waiting another week." Not that he wanted to wait. He just didn't want her to feel coerced into something she wasn't ready for.

Penelope frowned, looking down. "Oh. I thought you wanted to..." She was embarrassed that she'd brought it up if it wasn't something he wanted. She shouldn't have assumed...

"Oh, I do! I just don't want you to feel like I'm rushing you."

"I don't feel rushed at all. I feel like I've waited entirely too long."

He frowned for a moment thinking about the logistics of things. "I don't feel safe bringing you out on the prairie to sleep tonight, not with that man still roaming around, and with a storm coming. If we were really quiet though, we could make love in the tent tonight."

"I can be quiet!" she said.

"Then we'll do that." He took her hand and brought it to his lips. "You are making me the happiest man on earth. I feel gifted every time you even smile at me and making love with you will be a dream come true."

She moved closer to him again, wrapping her arms around him. "Thank you for supporting me through everything."

"You're my wife. What else would I do?"

As they walked back to camp together, she was both nervous and excited. Betty had given her good advice about this moment, and she was glad she wasn't going into it with just her mother's advice, which had been, "Close your eyes and think of the future of the country." *Ugh. That had not been helpful at all.*

When they were back at camp, Herb made quick work of putting up the tent. Everyone seemed to be sleeping, or getting close to sleep, so he immediately got into their small tent and waited for her.

As soon as she was in with him, he knelt in front of her, cupping her face in his hands. "I hope you know what a joy and a blessing you are to me. Every day a little more."

She smiled, a tear escaping her eye. This was so much different than it would have been with Reginald. Herb actually liked her for who she was, not for who he felt he could mold her into being.

His lips went to hers, and she put her arms around him, already knowing she loved the kissing part of marriage.

They slowly undressed one another, both of them reluctant to stop kissing, so it took much longer than it should have. Finally, when they were undressed and facing one another, the rain started pounding onto the oil cloth of the tent. And they were able to make love without worry someone would hear them.

Afterward, she lay in his arms, her head against his shoulder. "I feel like we should have done that on our wedding night," she said. "I'm sorry I made you wait."

"I offered to wait, if you'll recall." He kissed the top of her head. "Thank you for giving me the gift of yourself."

"And thank you for giving me the gift of you. All of you. You've been my fiercest protector, my helper, and my friend from the very beginning of this journey. I hope you know just how very much I appreciate all you've done."

During the night, the storm became stronger, and they dressed and climbed into the back of the wagon, amidst all of their belongings. They could see people around them doing the same. Storms like this made for rough travel, and she hoped it wouldn't last too long, but she was thankful she had stew left from the night before for them to eat if it did last a long time.

They had to sleep sitting up in the wagon, because there was so little room, but she pillowed her head against his shoulder, and they snuggled close.

When she woke it was well past dawn, but the rain was still coming down. "Is this going to delay us?" she asked.

Herb shook his head. "No, the captains have taken this sort of thing into account. We have a couple of weeks of rain days built into our schedule." That was the only thing the previous captain had been good about. Keeping them on schedule. Herb was thankful to him for that if for nothing else.

While in the wagon they talked, and she opened up about the full story about Muriel. "When I got the letter from her mistress, telling me that she'd had her whipped to death, I wept for days. I had to tell her mother, of course, and she threw herself on the floor, crying and screaming. My mother made her leave the house until she calmed down."

Herb shook his head. "That's terrible. I don't know how you were able to stay there for as long as you did."

"I didn't think I had a choice. I thought it was part of being obedient to my father in all things, like the Bible talks about.

Leaving...well, it seemed wrong, and I wouldn't have done it if I hadn't been expected to marry a man who was known for how poorly he treated his slaves and those around him. Rumor had it he beat his own mother for breaking a vase. A man like that would have been terrible to live with."

"Yes, he would have." Herb shook his head. "I'm so glad you got out when you did." He couldn't imagine her flesh bruised by the hand of the man who was supposed to take care of her and cherish her as they became one flesh.

"I am as well," she said, snuggling closer to him, glad the whole story was finally out. Well, everything was out except for the jewelry she had stashed in the flour sack, but that could wait.

The rain finally let up around noon, but when they got out of the wagon and looked around, everything was muddy, and the river had risen. "I have a feeling we won't be moving on today."

"We won't," Bob called from the next wagon over. "Applegate just made the decision."

"Thank you," Herb called back. "I think we should be thankful for the fresh water."

They ate the cold stew, and sat for a moment, just enjoying a time to rest and not having to constantly move. A short while later, people started coming to Herb to have repairs made on their wagons and their oxen reshoed while they were staying in place.

Herb made sure Mary was watching over Penelope before he left, though he worried about her.

Mary took the time to walk over and sit with Penelope. "I should go hunt, but I'm spending time with you instead." She looked cross to be taken from her favorite pastime.

"We certainly couldn't dry meat today. It's too wet."

"No, but we could provide fresh meat to a lot of the camp for their suppers tonight, which I think would please everyone."

"You're right," Penelope said. "Let's go hunt."

"Can you shoot?" Mary asked.

Penelope shook her head. "Herb is going to teach me, but it's been kind of busy around here."

"I'll teach you. We have the whole afternoon to hunt, because we can't move on with all this mud all over everything."

"I'd like that."

Mary got a pistol from the back of her wagon. "I like this for protection more than a musket." She held it up to show Penelope. "I'll teach you to use this, and you'll be able to keep it close. It's not nearly as heavy as my musket."

The two women went away from camp and Mary carefully scanned the area around them. "It's hard to have a target when there are so few trees, so I'm trying to find something else that would work."

She loaded the pistol and carefully showed Penelope each step of the process, before handing her friend the gun. "Do you see that knot in the grass?" she asked, pointing to a spot just about one hundred feet away.

Penelope nodded. "Yes."

"That's what I want you to aim for." Mary showed her how to point the pistol and line up her sight.

It took her four tries, but Penelope finally hit her target. Mary squealed with excitement. "You did it! Now hit it three more times, and then we'll find a new target."

They worked on shooting for hours, and Penelope's arm was aching by the time they were done.

"That's enough for now," Mary said, taking the pistol. "I'm confident you could do well enough to at least keep a man at bay."

Since that would be her only goal, Penelope knew she'd learned what she needed to learn. "I hope so," Penelope said. "Should we hunt now?"

"All that shooting has probably scared off every critter for a hundred miles," Mary said with a laugh. "We'll hunt another day."

Together the two women walked back to camp, and Penelope saw that Herb was waiting for her. "I have a surprise," he said with a smile.

"What's that?"

"I got a buffalo for supper. I've given away most of the meat, but there's enough left for our meal too."

"I sure hope you gave some to Bob. Mary's provided us with food a couple of nights in a row."

"I didn't because I was hoping you'd be willing to invite Bob and Mary over tonight. They've done so much lately that I want to thank them, and I get the impression Mary isn't overly fond of cooking."

Penelope smiled. "She doesn't seem to mind it too terribly much. I think she'd rather be hunting, but she'll cook when she needs to."

"Well, I'll go over and invite them if you don't mind."

"Not at all. I'm glad you thought of it."

Penelope looked through the dried fruit she had in the back of the wagon and found some cherries she hadn't realized were there. Most likely they'd been purchased by Herb for his journey and she just hadn't found them yet. She quickly took them out to make a cobbler from. She knew she'd seen a cobbler receipt in the cookbook.

By the time supper was ready, Mary and Bob had been there for a while visiting with Herb. Occasionally, Mary would help Penelope with something, but for the most part, she let her friend do the hard work of cooking alone. "I'll help with the dishes."

Penelope nodded. "Thank you for that, but you don't need to. This meal is our way of repaying you for your kindness." When she had finished, she put the food out for them. It was a simple meal with rice, gravy, and the buffalo meat cut up into chunks and served on top. There should be enough for their noon meal the next day as well, which thrilled Penelope. She liked being able to cook one meal and eat it twice.

While they ate, Mary told the men about teaching Penelope to shoot that day, and they all laughed at some of their mishaps. "I do feel like she could protect herself with a pistol easily now."

Herb grinned. "I planned to teach her, but I'm so glad you did it for me. I never seem to have time, and I do love my walks with my wife."

"I understand. Today there was nothing but time, so I showed her, and she's a quick study." Mary smiled at Penelope, who felt shy with the conversation being about her.

"I'll give you my pistol to start carrying tomorrow then."

"Thank you," Penelope said.

Mary shook her head. "She's new enough to shooting that I think she'll do better if she uses the same pistol. I'll give her that one to use until she's out of danger."

Herb nodded. "You're probably right. I hadn't thought of that."

When Penelope went to fetch the cobbler she'd made, Herb was excited. "Cherry cobbler? That's my favorite!"

"I found the dried cherries in the back of the wagon, and I didn't think you'd mind if I used them."

"You can use as many as you like to cook as long as you don't mind if I eat them!"

She laughed. "You know I don't." She gave everyone a plate before sitting down to get eat her own. "I hope it turned out all right. This is my first cobbler."

Herb was the first to take a bite, and he smiled, nodding. "Maybe a little more sugar next time, but I have a sweet tooth."

"I think it's perfect," Mary said. "Especially for your first time making a cobbler."

Penelope took a bite, and she found it a little too tart, just as Herb had. "I think Herb is right and it needs a little more sugar."

"I like things tart," Mary said.

Bob shook his head. "Doesn't surprise me at all."

They all laughed at that, and then got down to the serious business of eating the cobbler.

Mary was true to her word and helped with the dishes while the men sat and talked about protecting Penelope. It seemed to be a conversation that they'd had before.

"I say we just need to finish the man and bury him so he can't come back," Bob said.

"I don't think that's a good idea. More and more men will just be sent after her. No, I think we need to find a way to get it back to her father that she's married, so he'll leave her alone."

"Maybe," Bob said, but he sounded skeptical.

Penelope frowned, voicing her opinion for the first time. "I think Herb is right. My father is a very stubborn man, and he'll keep sending people to find me until someone lets him know I'm married and under someone else's protection." She didn't want to think about what the consequences would be with both her father and Reginald if she went back to Virginia.

"Maybe," Bob said, but he didn't sound convinced.

Of course, it didn't matter much what Bob thought about the whole situation. They would do what Herb thought was right since Herb was her husband. Thankfully. Bob and Mary seemed happy together, but Penelope couldn't imagine being married to anyone but Herb.

They didn't walk that evening, because the mud was too thick to enjoy it, but they were hopeful it would dry out enough they'd be able to be on their way the following day. They went into their tent that night and as they lay there in each other's arms, they talked about the future.

"I do think we'll settle near the others," Herb said, "and I'll set up a blacksmith's shop. It'll be good for the town and for us."

"And we'll get more land to homestead as a married couple," she added.

"Maybe we can let someone else use the land we don't need," he said.

"That could work. I want enough space for a kitchen garden, though. I think it would be nice to grow some of the food we eat."

"What did your family grow back in Virginia?"

"Cotton. Reginald grew Tobacco." Penelope frowned. "Those crops really do need extra hands to work to keep it up."

"I know they do. I'm glad I'm not someone having to make a decision about using slave labor or not."

She propped up on one elbow and looked down on him. "Do you think you would use slave labor?"

He thought for a moment, but finally shook his head. "No, I really don't think I would. Especially not with everything you said about Muriel."

Penelope was able to settle down then. "At least we agree." She was relieved she'd married a man with the same morals she had. It would make life easier for her.

Chapter Six

Thursday, June 4th, 1852

We are still traveling along the North Platte River. Yesterday's rain was a welcome respite from having to drive, and I'm thankful that we had it, though it will put us a day further from finding the elephant. I worry about Penelope and the man who is looking for her. She has learned to shoot, and she is a very capable woman, but I do not know what she will do when he returns. We must make him move along as quickly as we can.

Penelope was actually glad to be on their way again the following morning. Having a day off in the middle of the week had been nice, but the sooner they made it across the river, and the fewer rainstorms there were between now and that time, the safer they would all be.

She had started to really enjoy her time with the other women, and she could see that along with Betty, Katie and Mary were going to be special friends to her. It was odd feeling the weight of the pistol in the pocket of her apron as they walked, but it was a good odd. She felt protected.

Late into the afternoon, Katie grabbed her arm. "Several of us are going to help Mr. Simmons. His wife died a few weeks back, and his clothes were all washed downstream. Are you skilled with a needle?"

Penelope smiled. "I plan to open a dress shop when we reach Oregon. I have plenty of fabric in my wagon."

"Oh, wonderful. His little girl, Emily, needs some new dresses as well. Perhaps you could sew one of her dresses?" Katie seemed excited to be able to coordinate for the small family.

Penelope nodded. "I would enjoy that." She had always loved to sew, and she thought of the fabric packed in the back of the wagon as the beginning of her business. "I'll start on that this evening."

"I'll send Emily to your fire this evening for you to take measurements."

"Do you know what her favorite color is?" Penelope asked, thinking about the box where she'd stored the fabric. It was deep into the wagon, and she didn't want to have to climb back in there more than once.

"I don't. I'm sure you can ask her when she comes to see you this evening."

"I'll do that." Penelope was excited to get started. "What will you do when you reach Oregon?" She couldn't help but wonder what other women without husbands would do there.

Katie shrugged. "I am planning to homestead. That was the original plan when we started west, but after my husband's death I wasn't sure I'd be able to do it. But I feel stronger now, and I think between me and Stanley, we can figure things out."

"Good," Penelope said with a smile. "Are you settling near the rest of us?"

"I do believe I am. I feel like the people in this company are now my family, and if I can stay close to the rest of you, then I know I'll feel safe."

"So, does that make us sisters?"

Katie smiled. "I would *adore* having you for my sister."

When they stopped for the evening, Penelope made a simple meal of johnny cakes and bacon, glad they finally had an evening with no one joining them for their meal. Herb was perfectly content eating the breakfast foods for supper. "I appreciate you always doing such a good job cooking for me," Herb said.

She smiled, blushing a little. "I try hard. I know I'm not the best cook, but it's never because of lack of effort."

"I know that. I can tell you put your everything into what you do."

"I do." She finished eating and as she was washing the dishes, little Emily came into camp. Penelope hurried to the wagon and pulled out her measuring tape. Carefully, she measured the girl, jotting down what she needed to remember. "What is your favorite color, Emily?"

Emily scrunched up her face, thinking about it. "I like blue."

"All right. Thank you!" As soon as Emily had scurried away, she realized Herb had no idea why the little girl had even come to camp. "Emily and her father lost all their clothes in the storm yesterday. They were washed down river."

He shook his head. "I'm glad it was just clothes and not their food."

"I am as well. I did agree to make Emily a dress. Everyone is pitching in and making an item of clothing."

"That will be nice."

"I'm going to finish the dishes and then get started if you don't mind. I'm anxious to get it ready for her."

"So, you don't want to walk with me this evening?" he asked, frowning at her.

She made a face. "We could take a quick walk but let me find just the right fabric first." She climbed all the way into the back of the wagon and found her box of precious fabric. This was the last thing she'd want to lose in a sudden storm. She dug through the box and found a pretty light blue fabric that she knew would match the girl's eyes perfectly.

She put the cloth at the end of the wagon, but when she went to jump down, Herb caught her by the waist and lifted her to the ground. "Let's walk."

Penelope smiled. "Absolutely."

As they left camp, she talked to him about her day, explaining how everyone was coming together to help Mr. Simmons. "Emily lost her mother a few weeks back, so there's no one to sew for them. We all feel like a family, so I will sew for the girl. I'll help with her father's clothes as well if I'm needed of course."

"Of course." He smiled at her. "I didn't know you had so much fabric hidden away in the back of the wagon." He was thrilled she seemed to be prepared for what was to come.

She stopped walking for a moment, frowning. "I haven't told you my plans for when we reach Oregon?" she asked. "I want to start a dress shop. I plan on sewing for all of the women and children. I'm very excited about it."

He shook his head, a smile lighting up his face. "I had no idea. I think that's a great idea, but it might be good if you added in men to sew for. Men need work shirts."

"Well, that's true," she said, thinking about it. "I can add men in, but I will probably need to order some more fabrics in." The idea of ordering more fabric was even exciting. She simply loved everything about the idea of being a seamstress, even though she knew her mother would be mortified to think of her daughter working for others. Perhaps that was part of the draw. "What about you? Do you have any plans other than starting your blacksmith shop?"

He shook his head. "Well, I think I want to have a stable connected to it. I believe if I have a stable and breed some horses, as well as doing my blacksmithing, I'll make a great deal more money."

"Do you want to be a rich man?" she asked. She'd seen what wealth could do to people and thinking of Herb wanting to be wealthy was a little frightening.

He frowned at the question. "I don't want to be fabulously wealthy and have people waiting on my every whim, but I would like to make a good living for you and any children that may come along. My father was never rich, but I've never seen a happier man."

"Tell me about your parents," she said, taking his arm and snuggling against him as they walked. "You've told me very little about your past, and I've told you everything about mine."

"You didn't tell me until today that you wanted to own a dress shop."

She nodded. "I think I was afraid that if I spoke my desires aloud, I'd never be able to make them happen, if that makes any sense."

"I suppose it does."

"Your parents!" she reminded him.

"Oh, yes, well, my father is a blacksmith, and he taught me everything I know. He and my mother were childhood sweethearts. She came from a family of great wealth in New York City, and my father was just a blacksmith's son. As soon as they met, they fell in love, and for a time, her father told them they weren't allowed to court, but my mother kept talking to her mother and to her father, telling them what a wonderful man John, my father, was. Eventually, she wore them down, and they gave him some money to start a shop."

"Oh, I love this story!"

He chuckled. "My father tried to start a shop in New York, but there was just too much competition, so they decided to move to Missouri, knowing it was a place that was mostly unsettled at that time, and it would be a good place to start a business. So, after much forethought and planning and saving every day for a few years, they moved to Independence. Shortly after their arrival, I was born."

"Are you the youngest?" she asked.

"I'm an only child. Mother desperately wanted children, but she wasn't able to have them. Missouri ended up being the place where they needed to be for whatever reason. My parents still see one another, and their faces light up with love."

"They're going to miss you terribly." Penelope couldn't imagine her only child moving so far away from her.

"They are, but they understand that they followed their dreams and found the perfect place for them to live. Now I need to do the same for myself. I need to find my dreams, and I believe they lie in Oregon. It's like Missouri was when my parents settled there. It's a new area opening up and people will be needing the services of a blacksmith and a livery. I'll provide those services."

"So really, you're going west to fulfill all your dreams."

"I am in so many ways. I always wanted to marry and settle down, but I couldn't find anyone who I wanted to marry. As soon as I saw you, I knew that was changing."

She smiled at him. "I'm glad you felt that way and you kept pursuing me." She went into his arms and kissed him. "You are ten times the man Reginald was."

"The man you were to marry?" he asked.

"Yes, the man my father chose for me. He's wanted us to marry since I was a baby, and it's been dreadful keeping him waiting." She shook her head. "I probably shouldn't have waited as long as I did, but I don't care. I wanted to marry someone I could care for and respect. You're that someone."

He kissed her forehead before heading back toward camp. "Now let's talk about this dress shop of yours..."

"What do you want to say about it?" she asked, dreading the idea of him taking it over.

"I'm curious what you're thinking for it. What will you need to get it started?"

She shrugged. "I'll need a place to live first. I think for a good while, I can work at home, and then eventually I'll need a building, but that will take a while. Mostly I just want to be able to help with expenses. I was planning on that and renting my land being my whole income, but now I don't need to."

"We can still rent your land, but perhaps we should keep mine for the horses I want to raise. It might be smart for me to raise oxen as well. People will need them for plowing."

She nodded. "That could be very smart." She was excited he was talking about her portion of the land as if it would still be hers.

"We'll have to think on it. I like the idea of two of the stores in town having the name Jensen on them."

"What if I want my shop to be called Penelope's Dresses?"

"Then that's what it will be called. Your dress shop is your dream, and I will help you with ideas, but you'll get to make all the decisions. It's not my place to make those decisions for you."

"You'd really let me make the decisions?" she asked, a bit stunned. No one had ever allowed her to make her own decisions about anything. That was a big part of the reason she wanted to go west so badly.

"The decisions are yours to make. You need to follow your dream not mine. As I said, I'll make suggestions, but you don't have to agree with them. And I would love if you'd help me with suggestions. That's how my parents' marriage was. A partnership, and that's what I want from ours as well."

In that moment, her heart leapt. She'd known he was much better for her than her father or Reginald, but the idea that he would let her make her own decisions about business matters told her that she'd chosen to marry the right man.

As soon as they got back to camp, he erected their tent while she started the painstaking process of cutting out the dress she'd make for Emily. It wasn't easy to do on the ground, but she found a large piece of oil cloth she used to keep the fabric clean as she worked with it.

Just as it was getting to be too dark to see, she had the dress cut out and ready to sew. She'd spend every spare moment on it until it was done, and then see if she could make something else. Why, she could make a little money by taking in mending as they traveled. Perhaps her jewelry could be handed down to her daughter instead of having to be sold to start their businesses.

She still had no idea if Herb had anything saved, or if he was just going to do what he could with the land he received from the government, but it didn't matter much to her. She could help others, and so could he. That was what life was going to be about for them.

She carefully folded the dress pieces and put them in the back of the wagon, before climbing into the tent. Herb was lying on his side, sleeping soundly, and she snuggled into his arms, trying not to wake him.

His eyes opened and he rubbed a hand from her shoulder down to her wrist. "I think I'm needing to feel a little affection from my wife."

She laughed softly. "I was thinking along those lines, and I agree. A whole lot of affection would be nice tonight."

Penelope kissed him, her hands touching him in ways she didn't know if she should, but when he didn't stop her, she grew bolder. Her life was so much different than she'd imagined it would be after she'd married.

There were no slaves. She worked a great deal harder than she'd ever thought she would, but the work was good, and she was married to a good man. What more could a young lady ask for?

Afterward, Herb lay there while she fell asleep, thinking about what he could do to show his love for her. He didn't feel like they'd had enough time to just court, and he wanted to find a way to court his wife. There had to be something he could do to show her she was the most special woman he'd ever met.

It was hard with most days being the same on their journey, but there was a way. Maybe he should talk to her friend Betty or even Mrs. Gabriel. She seemed to understand Penelope in ways he didn't.

After breakfast the next morning, Herb went in search of Mrs. Gabriel. Hopefully, she would have some ideas for a nice romantic way for them to spend their evening.

"Mrs. Gabriel?"

The woman turned from her fire. "Yes, Mr. Jensen?"

"I was hoping for a little advice if you don't mind." He was embarrassed to be asking, but he needed a woman's perspective.

"Of course, I don't mind. What's troubling you?"

"I am looking for a way to court my wife. A way that will be easy on the trail. I want to show her a romantic evening tonight, but there will be no music, so we can't dance."

She smiled at him, nodding. "Pick her some flowers, tell her that she doesn't have to cook. I'll make a meal for you both, and you can pick it up on your way to see her."

"That's a good idea. I can pay you a penny for your troubles."

"No, I'm doing this as a friend. Then take her on a long walk by the river. Talk to her and tell her your feelings."

Herb's eyes widened. "She's not ready to hear my feelings."

Mrs. Gabriel laughed. "I've seen how she looks at you. Trust me. She's ready to hear whatever you want to say."

As Herb walked away from her, he wandered back to Penelope. "Don't cook supper tonight," he said.

Penelope frowned at him. "Why not? We need to eat."

"I've made other arrangements," he said, and then he went to hitch up the team.

Penelope stared after him, wondering what he was planning. It was something, and she wanted to know. She'd never been good at waiting for surprises. She'd always wanted to know what was going to happen early.

As soon as they were on their way, Penelope fell into line with the other women. She felt excited to know what was happening with their supper that evening. Whatever it was, she'd have a little more time to work on Emily's dress. She had two of the pieces with her as they walked, and she worked on basting them. It wasn't the easiest thing she'd ever done, walking and sewing, but it would be worth it to have it done as quickly as she possibly could.

Emily skipped along beside her, looking at the fabric in her hands. "Is that my dress?"

Penelope nodded. "Do you like the color?"

"Yes! That's the prettiest blue in all the world." Emily spread her arms wide.

"I think so too," Penelope said with a smile. "I hope you'll be happy with your dress."

"I want a pretty dress with a skirt that goes out around me."

"I'm not sure if a hoop skirt would be good for a girl your age on the trail..." Penelope was certain it wouldn't, actually, but she didn't want to crush the girl either.

"Oh. Well, if you don't think I should have them, then that will be fine. Maybe when we get to Oregon you could make me a hoop skirt."

Penelope laughed. "Maybe I will. We'll talk to your father about that when we get closer."

By the time they stopped for lunch, she'd managed to baste the pieces together. It was something she could have sewed in an hour normally, but while walking the slow pace of the oxen, it was a lot more time consuming. But what a good way to use her time and not worry about the walking they were constantly doing.

For lunch, they had cold johnny cakes from the night before, and she sat on a quilt on the ground with some of the other women, and Herb joined her. She had two more pieces of the dress ready to baste while she ate, and she hoped to use the time they were allotted to rest after the noon meal to work on the dress as well.

"That's coming along," Herb said, nodding to the pieces of dress in her hand.

"It will as long as I have time to work on it," she said with a smile. "I do look forward to having it finished for Emily."

"Just think, once we're in Oregon, you'll get to sew even more. Do you think you'll specialize in day dresses or nice dresses for parties?"

"I hope to do a little of both," she responded.

Hannah seemed to pick up the conversation. "Are you planning to start a dress shop, Penelope?"

"I am. I'm actually really excited about it. I've always enjoyed sewing and needlepoint." She didn't add that she'd been taught to sew by a slave whose daughter had been her closest friend and confidante, because that was knowledge no one needed. And it still hurt to think of Muriel.

"You do beautiful work," Hannah said, lifting a portion of the pieces. "Your stitches are so straight and perfect. Mine are always a little crooked. My mother gave up trying to teach me to do better. I was a lost cause."

Penelope laughed. "I have always enjoyed it a great deal, and my mother would make me sit with her for hours every day doing needlepoint. I'm not quite as fond of needlepoint as I am of sewing, but I still enjoy it. I like to make little flowers on sleeves of my dresses." She showed Hannah her sleeve. She'd never been allowed to make her own clothes, because that was not work for a lady, but she'd made several dresses for the slaves of the plantation. Just never where her mother would see her.

"Oh, that flower is beautiful. I would love you to do something like that for me."

"I would enjoy that." Penelope smiled. "I'm going to finish this first, though."

"I'm in no hurry. I just think it would be fun to have something like that." Hannah shrugged. "Maybe a pastor's wife shouldn't be so vain as to want flowers on her sleeves."

"There's nothing wrong with it," Penelope assured her. "Back in Virginia, our pastor's wife wore silks to church every week. She wore what she was given by the wives of her husband's congregants, and they all wore silks." She remembered her mother once telling her that a lady must never be seen in the same dress twice. It had seemed ridiculous at the time, and it seemed even more ridiculous now.

"I think that would be lovely," Hannah said, smiling. "I have a feeling I won't be given cast off silks in Oregon, though."

"No, but perhaps if you'd like, Herb and I could tithe with clothing for you."

Herb jerked against her and she looked at him, not quite understanding what was wrong. She would need to be sure to ask him later.

"I'd like that a lot. Or I can just give you dresses to embroider. Either way. I'm excited to have a dressmaker that will be a part of our little community."

"I hope I live up to expectations." Penelope was surprised that anyone would show an interest already, but she was pleased. And she decided she would embroider something small and pretty on Emily's dress. The girl would be a walking advertisement for her.

As they finished their break, and Penelope went back to the wagon to get more pieces to baste, she asked Herb what had bothered him about her offering to tithe with a dress.

"I feel like it'll be my responsibility to feed and clothe us and tithe." Herb frowned at her. "I like the idea of you having a business, but not if you use it just to pay the bills."

She sighed. "What will I use it for then? The money you make will be our money, so the money I make will be our money as well, won't it?"

"I never thought of it that way," he said. "I suppose that's true."

"Good, then don't worry about things like that. There's enough going on in our lives to worry about. Don't you think?"

He nodded. "You're right. Are you still wearing your apron and keeping the pistol in your pocket?" he asked.

"I am. I won't let anyone come near me. I promise."

"Good." He smiled at her, kissing her forehead. "I hate that I can't watch over you every second."

"I don't need to be watched every second. I'm doing just fine. The other women are there, and Mary always has her musket."

"Then I will stop borrowing trouble and start driving toward Oregon."

She smiled. "We'll get there much faster that way."

Chapter Seven

June 5, 1852

I love that I have something to work toward on this never-ending journey of ours. Making a dress for a little motherless child has made me feel as if I'm doing something good with my time and not just plodding along toward a place that might never appear. It makes me feel good about myself that I have a skill that's needed by someone.

All of my life I've been told to sit down and look pretty, but there's more to me than looking pretty, and people are starting to see that finally. I feel blessed that I've stepped into this new world full of people who have to fight for everything they have and don't have things handed to them on a silver platter. I feel like I belong here so much more than I ever felt as if I belonged at home. I feel as if I've found where I belong, and it's wherever this wonderful group of people that I'm with is. Whether it's in a camp in Independence, Missouri or in the middle of the great plains somewhere. I'm where I should be.

By suppertime, Penelope was very curious about whatever it was Herb had planned, but she used her time wisely to continue basting the dress for little Emily. As she sat working on it, Emily came to visit again. "Will this be my skirt?"

"It will. Do you like it?" Penelope held it up for the little girl to see.

"I wish there were butterflies on it," Emily said, looking sad.

"Do you like butterflies?"

"I love them. My mama always said butterflies were the best of all insects, because they look pretty, and they help make flowers grow."

Penelope smiled. "Your mother sounds like a *very* smart woman."

"She was very smart," said a young girl who must have been around fifteen. She was odd looking with a peppermint stick coming out of the top of her dress. "I liked her. She taught me how to make a couple of things over the fire. Someday, I'm going to be the best cook in all of the world!"

Penelope nodded. "And you are?"

The girl pulled the peppermint stick from her cleavage and sucked on one end of it. "I'm Edna Blue. People think I'm strange, but I just understand a lot of things. I think you and your new husband are going to make beautiful children." With that the girl walked away.

Penelope looked at Emily. "Do you think she's odd?"

Emily nodded emphatically. "Yes, but she's nice, so it's all right by me that she's a little strange." Emily hurried off to play, and Penelope eyed the fabric she was using.

It was a solid color fabric, and Penelope knew she could easily add a butterfly or two. She smiled as she thought about just where they should go.

She was so involved in her dressmaking that she didn't notice when Herb came up to their fire and presented her with a beautiful bouquet of wildflowers. "Where did these come from?" She hadn't even noticed any flowers around to pick.

He smiled. "I found them after I saw to the livestock."

She took the flowers from him and inhaled deeply of their aroma. "They're beautiful. Thank you for being such a thoughtful husband."

"You wait there. I'll be right back."

Penelope thought the man was acting odd, but she didn't mind. She went back to her sewing, determined to have the dress done before services on Sunday afternoon. She knew that Emily would be very proud to wear her new butterfly dress to church.

When Herb returned, there was a large pot dangling from his hand with a wonderful smell emanating from it. "Where did you get that?" she asked, more than a little surprised.

"Mrs. Gabriel agreed to make supper, so you could have an evening off from cooking," he said. He opened the pot and his taste buds sat up to take notice. Apparently, Mrs. Gabriel was a wonderful cook.

"It smells so good."

"I have a feeling it will taste even better," he said. He set the pot down and got them each a dish, serving up the rice and the bits of meat cooked through it.

When she stood up to help, he waved her away. "No, I'm doing for you tonight."

She smiled, surprised that he was acting so infatuated. He'd never been this way with her before. "Thank you."

"You're very welcome," he said. He handed her a plate with her food on it as well as a fork, and they both ate. "I'm hoping to take you on a walk this evening. I know you're working on the dress, but I think a nice romantic walk along the river is what we both need." He really needed her to agree for the rest of the evening he had planned. He was surprised just how much he was enjoying courting her this way.

"It sounds lovely."

He washed the dishes while she sewed, and she wanted to laugh at how ineptly he did it. He was definitely not used to washing dishes any more than she was.

As soon as he was finished, she put her sewing into the back of the wagon, and she took his arm to walk with him. As they strolled through camp, she realized they'd done the same thing just a week before, surprising everyone. Now no one thought a thing of it. Were they an old married couple now? She didn't know, but she did know she enjoyed walking with him a great deal. Well, she enjoyed everything she did with him. It was strange just how much fun she had when they were together.

As they walked, he told her how pretty she was, and she blushed. "You already have me as a wife, Herb. You don't need to try to court me."

"That's the thing," he said. "I never had a chance to court you because we married so quickly, but I don't want you to look back at your life and be sad you weren't properly courted by your husband. So, I'm going to do my best to make up for it." He hoped his explanation would tell her how very much she meant to him.

"I see that." She smiled up at him. "I could never feel like I missed out on anything with you beside me, Herb. You've truly helped me feel like I belong in this camp, and I know without a doubt that I belong in your arms."

He smiled at her words, stopping then and leaning down to kiss his wife. They were still within sight of camp, and he rarely kissed her where people could see, but in that moment, it felt right. "And I feel like my arms belong around you."

She grinned. "Well, then we're both happy, aren't we?"

"Definitely. I never imagined I could feel this happy." He struggled for the right words as they began walking again. "My whole life I've been watching my parents and praying every night that God would send me a woman I could love the way my father loved my mother. And then I saw you in Independence, and I knew you were the woman I'd been praying for."

She sniffled as a tear touched her cheek. "You say the most wonderful things, Herb. I'll be praying that my daughters will someday marry a man just like you. A man who can make them feel loved and cared for in any situation." She didn't know what she'd done to deserve a man like him, but she was so glad to have him.

"Do you really feel that way?" he asked.

"Of course, I do. You brought me flowers, arranged to have supper made, and you brought me for a walk and told me so many wonderful things. How could I feel anything but loved with you around?" She shook her head. "When I was a girl, my tutor would tell me about the knights of the round table, and I would listen with rapt attention. I decided then that I wouldn't marry until I found my own knight. It was a silly thing to decide, and I was young, so you have to forgive that...but I do feel like you are the knight I spent my whole life looking for. You're the man who God made just for me." She rested her head on his shoulder for a moment. "Thank you for coming into my life and changing the wheel on my wagon a week ago. Do you realize everything changed that day?"

He smiled. "I do, and I think it's a good thing. I will do everything I can to make sure you feel like we're courting."

"I appreciate that. But then I appreciate all you do for me every day. I hope you know that."

He nodded. "I do. And I will try to change my thinking about how we use the money you earn with your dress shop. I hope you're not one of those women who wants to have a huge house with servants."

"Not at all. I lived with that as a child, but as an adult, I want to see things around me that were purchased with things I earned myself."

"And things I earned?" he asked.

"Of course. Anything one of us earns we both do." She smiled up at him, and then looked out over the river. "How long until we cross?"

"As soon as we can. We should be able to cross within a week from what I understand."

"Are you worried?" she asked, sensing something in his voice.

"Conversations like this are not what I was expecting when I took you for a long romantic walk."

"Please, Herb. I know there's something you're not telling me."

"The rainstorm may make it harder than it would have been to cross, and this and a place called Bear River are the two most dangerous crossings we'll have on the entire journey." He shook his head. "I'll be taking the wheels off each wagon and reassembling them on the other side. No one is going to risk me in any way, but many men have been lost on this crossing."

She frowned up at him. "So, any of my friends could lose her husband here?"

"Any of them. I know it's not what you want to hear, and I don't want to say it. Thankfully, we have a good doctor and a good preacher with us on this journey. I think we're going to be all right."

"I'll still worry. How could I not?"

He sighed. "And this is why I didn't want to have this discussion with you."

"Well, now that we've had it, what can I do to help lower the risk?"

"Not a thing," he said. "You'll need to stay out of the way. We may have to build canoes to get across or the company in front of us may leave some behind, but whatever it takes, that's what we'll do."

Penelope nodded, taking a deep breath. "Are we worried about the oxen?"

He shrugged. "I'm not nearly as worried about losing oxen as I am about losing people. There are plenty of oxen. No human life is worth less than the best of the oxen."

She stood looking out across the river, which looked so calm there to her. "Couldn't we cross here? Now, where it's calm?"

"There are undercurrents here. The safest place to cross is still a few days walk from here. We'll make sure we cross at the safest place. I promise." He wrapped his arms around her from behind, standing and staring out over the water with her.

"And you promise not to be noble and risk your life for someone else's?"

"I promise that I will do my best to survive no matter what. You and any children we may have keep me motivated to keep going every day."

"What have I done in my life to deserve marriage to a man like you?" she asked, finally voicing what she'd been thinking.

"You were born. That's enough for me. You have the kindest heart of anyone I've ever known. Your story about Muriel is enough to tell me that."

She nodded. "I would have brought Muriel with me if she was still alive. I don't care what anyone said. She deserved to be a free woman."

"Tell me about her."

She leaned back against him as she let the memories wash over her. Now, with the sun setting and in this beautiful place on the river, she knew it was the right time to talk about her friend. "She loved to play tricks on me. Not big tricks, but silly little things to make me laugh. One day, I looked at my school paper, and she'd written her name on top of it, and crossed mine out. She understood arithmetic much better than I ever could, and she would help me with my numbers every day." She shook her head. "My mother liked to tell me that slaves were like animals, and we should treat them that way, but no animal could ever do sums in his head the way Muriel did. And she loved to tell stories. I think she heard them from her mother. She would tell stories of what it was like back in Africa, and what the ocean crossing was like in chains. I know someone had to tell her about them, but when she told me, I could almost see her there, chained below deck with the rest of her people."

"She sounds like a very special person."

"Oh, she was. And when we played games together, she *never* let me win. I would hear her mother tell her that the whites always had to win, but she refused to put up with that. And she was pretty. She had the most beautiful eyes you've ever seen. So dark and soulful." Penelope sighed. "It feels good to talk about her. Even after she died, my mother wouldn't let me speak of her, and she had Muriel's mother sent to the fields to work, so I couldn't talk to her either. Everyone wanted me to pretend that she had never existed, and I just couldn't do that. Not at all."

He pulled her closer against him, his hands moving up and down her arms. "It sounds to me like you really loved her." He didn't know many women who could love a slave with everything inside them the way she did. She was a miraculous woman in so many ways.

"Of course, I did. I once asked my mother if she was my twin, because we were born on the same day, and we both nursed from the same woman. It made my mother very angry."

"I'm sure it did. Tell me about your mother."

Penelope sighed. "She was...well, she was the perfect Southern lady. She did as she was told when she was told. She never thought for herself except where her jealousy over me was concerned. She hated Mabel, that was Muriel's mother's name, with everything inside me for stealing me away from her." She shook her head. "I never felt that Mabel was my mother, though. She was Muriel's mother, but I did love her very much. Mabel is a good woman."

"You said you have a brother, right?"

"I have a younger brother. He's being groomed to be the same type of man my father is. Seth is his name. He's twelve, and he truly is a good person...until he spends time around Father. I told him about Muriel and explained it all. He held my hand while I cried. And then Father filled his head with lies about how slaves aren't really people, and he came to me and told me it was time for me to grow up and stop talking about a dead slave." She shook her head. "I think in a year or two, he will be unrecognizable.

"That's terrible. I'm so sorry!"

"I went and saw Mabel the day I left. I gave her the engagement ring Reginald had given me. I knew I would never want to look at it again, and it could help her. I told her to get away and sell it so she could be free. I don't know if she did it, but I hope so."

Herb smiled at that. "Here you are, starting a small revolution all on your own. You really are a rebel, little wife."

She laughed. "I try to do what's right. If that makes me a rebel then I can very proudly say that's exactly what I am. Slavery needs to be ended, and it needs to happen yesterday. No one should own another person that way. It's not right! And I think if the slaves want to return to Africa and go back to living the way they lived there, they should be allowed to do so, and they should be given free passage on a ship back. I'm not sure it could work that way, but it should."

"I see you have very strong opinions about this."

"I do. Do you have strong opinions about anything?"

"I have strong opinions about the rights of women. I don't think you should have ever been told you had to marry a man you didn't love. You should have had that choice. That's one of the reasons the west is so appealing to me. I want to be able to live in a land where I know my daughters will be allowed to own land and be people in their own rights."

"I like that opinion," Penelope said with a grin. "Do you know Margaret Prewitt's story?"

"No, I don't. I know she was a widow." He wasn't sure what Margaret had to do with their discussion.

"Yes, her husband of six years died, and left her with Amanda and Sally, but his land immediately went to his closest male relative, so she wasn't even allowed to stay and attempt to farm on her own. Instead, she had to find a new place to live. She thought about moving herself and her girls back into her parents' home, but they made it clear they would be looking for a husband for her. She wasn't ready to marry, so she decided to come west instead. She sold everything she had of value so she could buy the oxen and the wagon."

"That's the kind of thing I mean! Women should have the right to own land. If you hadn't had a brother, what would have happened to your father's land when you died?"

"Reginald," she spat. "His father and my father have been close friends for years, and when I was born, they started talking about a wedding between us."

Herb frowned. "So, you've known you were supposed to marry him your entire life?"

"I have. And I have never liked it. Not one little bit. As a child, he was a bully. He would push me down and steal my dolls. When we were engaged, my mother told me I had to start letting him kiss me, and I just kept turning my cheek. There was no way his lips were going to touch mine." She shook her head. "No matter how many times I told my mother how mean Reginald was, she would just tell me I had to obey my father."

"I'm glad he never kissed you. I don't want to have to kill him."

She laughed. "You are a silly man. Neither of us are ever going to Virginia to kill anyone."

"You're right, but I could dream about it."

"Let's head back," she said. "I love it that you're courting me so sweetly, but I need to work on that dress a little more." She turned in his arms and kissed him. "Thank you for wooing me. I didn't realize how special something like this would feel."

He bowed low over her hand, kissing her knuckles. "Would you accompany me to the dance on Saturday night?"

"Oh, must I choose between that and laundry? I'm not sure I can make such a difficult decision..."

"This is one decision I will make for you. You are coming to the dance with me, and that's that."

"Well, if you're taking the decision out of my hands, I must conform to your husbandly wishes." She tried not to smile as she thought about avoiding laundry for several hours while she had fun.

He offered her his arm with a flourish. "Now I know how to get my way with you."

"Has that been a problem so far in our marriage?"

"Well, no, but there will come a day, I'm certain..." The grin he gave her let her know he was only joking. She liked this lighthearted side of him. It was something she'd rarely seen before.

When they got back to camp, he got his Bible out of the back of the wagon and read to her from Proverbs thirty-one. "This will teach you to be a good wife to me."

"If I'm not already there, I'm afraid I'm probably not going to improve a great deal."

"Quiet and listen, wife."

"I'm listening!"

And he read, verse after verse, and she listened, looking for ways she could be a better wife to him. She knew he was joking, but he'd been everything she'd needed since the day she'd met him, and she wanted to provide him with what he needed in a wife as well.

As she sewed together the bodice of the little dress, she thought about where her butterflies would need to go, and she decided one right in the front, and then a smaller one on each sleeve. If she worked late into the night by lamplight, she could have it done in time for the dance on Saturday.

As soon as Herb was done reading, she asked if he would mind if she stayed up late and worked by lanternlight.

"On the dress? Is there a hurry?"

"I'd like to have it ready for Emily to wear to the dance tomorrow night. She is so excited about it, and she just lost her mother...I guess I want to make her feel better in the only way I know how."

"Then I don't mind at all. Would you like me to sit up with you?" he asked.

"No but thank you. You need your rest, and I'm being silly pushing myself to get it done."

He leaned over and kissed her cheek as he walked toward the tent. "Not silly at all. You're being a caring person, and I think it's one of your very best qualities."

Penelope sat beside the fire and kept sewing as fast as her fingers would go, thinking about her husband's words, and realizing they were true. She did care. Perhaps too deeply sometimes, but she truly cared about everyone around her.

It was why she hadn't been able to tolerate cruelty in any way. Why she had hated slavery with everything inside her. She cared about the slaves as much as she cared about her own people. Why wouldn't she? They were humans too.

She was certain if everyone had a similar experience to the one she'd had, where she had gotten to know a slave so personally, they would all feel the same. And she wondered if she wrote out her experience and tried to have a newspaper publish it, after they were in Oregon, if perhaps it might make a difference in the way some people looked at slaves. If it did, maybe she could truly do something about the horrors she'd seen.

If not, it would only cost her a few hours' time and lots of tears to get it all on paper. She'd ask Herb for his opinion the next day, but as she sat and sewed, she could see her hand on the paper, and she thought about the exact words she would use.

"I was the daughter of a slave owner, and the best friend of a slave. I suckled at the breast of a woman who was born in Africa. I lost the sister of my heart when I was ten, when my father decided we were too close, and he sold her to another man. Sold her simply to get her out of my life.

"In the years since I have been without my sweet Muriel, I have thought about how similar we are. There were two differences between me and my friend. She and I were both owned in much the same way by my father. But she had dark skin, whereas mine is light. And she was of a different station in life. She was supposed to wait on me, and I was supposed to allow it. And I did allow it some of the time.

"She was just as bright, if not brighter than I was. I taught her to read and to do arithmetic. She taught me to sew. I taught her how to write her name. And she taught me how to truly love another person as much as is possible in our fleshly bodies. I will always miss my friend, Muriel, and I hope that after you hear her story, you will understand my hatred of the evil practice of slavery that half of our nation participates in. I hope you will tell everyone who will lend their ear about how people of African descent are the same as we are.

"And more than anything, I hope you will join me in praying for my sweet friend Muriel's soul."

Chapter Eight

Saturday June 6th, 1852

I have decided to forgo my place playing my fiddle with the others for the Saturday night dances until I know my wife is safe. She means so much more to me than any instrument ever could. I must watch over her as long as I know this threat is hanging over her. I expect Mr. Bradford to be back for her at any time, and I pray no one in our camp will let on that she's here.

We hope to cross the river on Monday, if no rains come before then. We will be at the safe crossing place tonight, but we may have to wait out storms or wait for the river to go down for a day or two. The weather looks clear, and Mr. Applegate says that his Farmer's Almanac predicts clear skies for the next few days. I pray the almanac is right.

Penelope sewed while she cooked breakfast on Saturday morning, and she spent the day sewing as she walked. She'd been able to embroider the pieces of the butterfly in place by lamplight the previous evening, and she was working on hemming the project. She desperately wanted Emily to be able to wear it for the dance that evening, and her fingers moved as quickly as they could to finish.

While they ate their cold lunch, her fingers sewed. While her husband rested beside her, she kept going. She talked to the other women, many of whom were working on projects for Emily or her father, while she worked, and it was a pleasant way to pass the time as much of the camp snoozed around them.

Finally, as they finished their day's trek, she made the last stitch, with barely no time to spare. She held up the dress to look at it critically, but she found nothing that bothered her. It was perfect.

She went to the wagon to start their fire for the evening, and Emily came over. "What are you cooking?" the little girl asked. She peered at the fire curiously.

"I'm making some beans and rice tonight, but I put a little bacon in with the beans to make them taste better." Penelope felt dejected at the very idea of eating beans again, but she was sure it was worse for the little girl. She wasn't sure if Emily's father could even cook.

Emily sighed dramatically. "I'm sick of eating beans."

Penelope leaned toward the little girl. "Do you want to know a secret?"

Emily nodded, her eyes excited. "What?"

"I didn't like beans even before we left Independence, and I hate them even more now." Penelope made a face.

Emily giggled. "That's not a secret. That's just a fact."

"That's true. Do you want to know a *real* secret then?"

Emily nodded. "Yes!"

"I finished your dress."

The little girl squealed and clapped her hands. "Where is it?"

Penelope went to her wagon and got the dress from the back of it, holding it up. "I just like how it turned out so much I think I might have to keep it and wear it myself."

"It's too little!" Emily walked over and carefully studied the dress. "There are butterflies," she said in a whisper.

"I thought a few butterflies would be good so you could always remember to pray for your mama. What do you think?"

Emily hugged both Penelope and the dress. "It's the most beautiful dress I've ever seen."

"I'm so glad you like it. Do you want me to help you put it on?" Penelope asked, thrilled with how the little girl was reacting to the dress she'd worked so hard on.

"Yes, please."

When Emily was wearing the pretty new dress, she spread her arms to both sides and spun in a circle, and her skirt swirled out around her. "You did make me a pretty skirt that spreads out when I spin!"

Penelope nodded. "I tried to make exactly what you wanted."

"I have to go and show my papa."

"Of course, you do!"

Trudie walked over then, smiling down at the little girl as she ran off. "That's the only kid in the whole camp I can tolerate. She's just so sweet, I can't imagine *anyone* not liking her."

"She is very sweet," Penelope said. "How was your day?"

"It was good. Very long, but good. I'm ready to rest tonight and tomorrow. This day off is something I look forward to all week."

"As do I!" Penelope looked at her. "Would you like to go to the dance with Herb and I this evening? You don't have to dance, but it's fun to enjoy the music."

Trudie frowned. "No one wants me at the dance."

"I do. I think we could become friends with just a little bit of effort," Penelope said. "I would love to have a chance to sit and listen to the music with you and just get to know you better."

"I told you, I'm not answering any questions about my past." Trudie crossed her arms over her chest, making it clear her stance wasn't about to change.

"Then I'll only ask questions about the present and future," Penelope said automatically. She could see Trudie needed a friend, but she would need to be met on her own terms.

"I guess that's all right then." Trudie didn't seem convinced, but Penelope was pleased she'd agreed. "I should go and fix myself some supper."

"I made enough to feed an extra mouth if you care to join us."

Trudie looked torn. "No, I should eat alone. If I'm around people too long, I get snappy, and no one needs to see that."

"All right." Penelope watched Trudie walk away, and while she wondered what the other woman was hiding, she didn't feel the need to ask. She knew that Trudie had her reasons for not talking about her past, and whatever they were, they were valid.

When Herb joined her a short while later for their meal, he asked if she was excited about the dance.

"Of course," she said. "Trudie is going to sit with us. She wants to go, but she doesn't want anyone asking her any questions."

"What do you think she's so secretive about?" he asked.

"I have no idea. I wonder, like you do, but I'm not going to speculate or try to figure it out." Penelope felt the need to respect the other woman's privacy.

"I think that's wise." He accepted the bowl she handed him. "I'm glad you're befriending her. I know how hard it is for her to trust anyone not to pry too much."

"It is, but she's got her right to privacy." Penelope didn't want the whole world to know that she ran away from an engagement, so she understood that the other woman probably had something in her past she didn't want to share.

"Just as you do," he said softly. "Will you wear your pistol to the dance tonight?"

"Of course, I will. It's how I keep myself safe after all."

"I'm there to keep you safe," he reminded her. He wondered for a brief moment if she trusted him.

"I know you are. But I like to do for myself as much as I can."

"I know you do. I'm pleased you're wearing it because I might need to step away for a moment."

"Good. Because I plan to wear it until I no longer feel as if I'm in danger."

"I think that's a really good idea," Herb said. "Beans for supper?"

She nodded. "We haven't had them in over a week, and I hate beans, so I need to spread them out as much as we can."

He laughed. "I didn't know you hated beans. They're a staple for this trip." There was no other way to survive than eating beans.

"They are, and I'm making them, and I'll pretend they're something else with every bite." Penelope sighed as she looked into the pot. "I wish there was a way to make them taste better."

"Perhaps you should take some time to talk to Margaret Prewitt about that. She did some wonderful things with spices for beans." He shrugged. "She's a really good cook, and I'm certain she wouldn't mind sharing some of her secrets."

"I'll do that. Maybe she can help me not hate them any longer."

"I think everyone on this journey will hate them by the end," he said, accepting the bowl of beans she handed him. "They look delicious."

She wrinkled her nose and sat beside him. "I suppose I should be happy that I have food, right? Back home, we always had delicious meals. Now that I'm expected to cook them, it's just not the same."

As they ate, she told him about Emily's reaction to the dress she'd made, and he smiled. "You put butterflies on it? I didn't even notice you doing that." He wondered if she had any idea just how miraculous he found everything about her, including her way to help a little girl remember the love she had for her mother.

"That's because I worked most of the night to put them on there while you slept," she said. "When you see her in it, you'll have to tell me what you think."

After she finished the dishes, they headed to the big open area in the middle of the campsite where they would have their church service the next day, but tonight, it would be where the music would be played and where the entire company would dance. Many of the women wore their fanciest dresses, and many of the men wore their best suits. Penelope was too tired to change, but she vowed she would for the next music night.

They all tired of wearing the same clothes day in and day out, so they made sure they enjoyed themselves on the one night a week set aside for pleasure.

They sat on a long bench that had been carved by a previous company, that looked weathered. It was probably built a few years before, but not too many, because people hadn't been traveling this way for long, except maybe Indians, and the Indians didn't usually sit on things. The ground worked well enough for them.

The musicians were just tuning up, and Jamie Prewitt, Margaret's husband, called out to them. "You should join us again soon, Herb. It's not the same playing without you."

"Hopefully, I'll be back next week!" Herb called back, putting his arm around Penelope's shoulders.

Trudie came to sit on the other side of Penelope, and she smiled at her. "I hadn't been here for the music before last week. It's fun to watch people dance and to join in if you feel like it."

"I won't be joining," Trudie said, "but I'll watch and enjoy the music." She had a faraway look in her eyes.

"Have you been to many dances?" Penelope asked.

"That's a question about my past. Why don't you ask if I plan to go to a lot of dances in the future?" Trudie smiled to let Penelope know she wasn't angry, but she was simply not going to answer that type of question, which was good enough for Penelope.

"Do you think you'll enjoy this dance?" Penelope asked, grinning at Trudie.

"I'm going to do my very best," Trudie responded.

As others started to join them, Emily brought her father, whom she was dragging by his hand. "Papa, this is Mrs. Jensen. She made my blue butterfly dress." Emily was wearing the dress, and Penelope had been right. It matched her eyes perfectly.

Trudie smiled at the child. "Oh, look at that dress. The stitchwork is amazing." She looked at the tiny butterflies adorning it. "I can't imagine anyone who could do better."

"It's the prettiest dress in the whole world," Emily said. "Watch!" She spun in a circle and the skirt swirled out around her.

Trudie clapped her hands. "The prettiest dress for the prettiest little girl in the world."

Penelope smiled at the sad looking man. "It's nice to meet you, Mr. Simmons. If there's anything I can do for you, let me know." She couldn't imagine the grief he must be going through, added to the responsibility of being both mother and father to a girl Emily's age. It had to be overwhelming.

He shook his head. "Thank you, though. I believe I have some new clothes being made now."

"And for your meals? How are you handling those?" Penelope asked, determined to invite them to eat with them if there was no one else doing that for them.

"I'll take care of their meals from now on," Trudie said, surprising Penelope. "Emily is my favorite little girl in all the world, after all. That makes it my place to help them."

"Of course, it does," Penelope said, smiling at her friend.

"I can't ask for charity," Mr. Simmons said, holding up a hand.

Emily groaned. "Papa, you don't know how to make anything but beans. *Please* let Miss Trudie help us."

Mr. Simmons looked down at his daughter. "It's enough that we let the nice ladies make clothes for us."

Trudie shook her head at Mr. Simmons. "I'm not offering you charity. I'm offering to cook the food you have for you, and I will eat it with you. It's just a way to help out, since I'm already cooking anyway. It's as easy to cook for three as it is for two."

He frowned for a moment and finally nodded. "That would be fine. Just be certain that you let us know if we become a burden."

Emily squealed and hugged her father and then Trudie. "Thank you thank you thank you. If you had ever eaten food Papa made, you'd understand why we need help so badly."

Trudie laughed, her face lighting up with the hug. "I'm happy to help you. We'll have to talk, and you can tell me your favorite trail foods, and I'll try to cook them as much as I can."

"No beans!" Emily said.

"I'll have to cook beans sometimes," Trudie told her, "but I'll try not to make them too much."

"I guess that will be all right," Emily said, taking her father's hand and dragging him away.

Penelope smiled at Trudie. "That was very kind of you to offer to help them that way."

Trudie shrugged. "I really do like Emily. She's such a sweet little thing. Having her at my fire every evening may make it so I'm not always in such a sour mood."

Penelope wanted to ask more questions, but she knew she shouldn't. It wasn't the right time. Perhaps there never would *be* a right time. "Did you know many of the people of our company are planning to settle near each other once we reach Oregon and find a good place?"

Trudie shook her head. "I had no idea."

"Perhaps you'll move near us as well. We'll have a preacher, a doctor, a blacksmith, and I'll be opening a dress shop. What more could you need in life?"

Trudie smiled. "I think I may do that. You are the first person I've been able to call a friend in a long while."

"I'm glad you call me friend, because that's exactly how I think of you," Penelope said.

The music started then, making it harder to talk, but Penelope was thrilled that her discussion with Trudie had gone so well. She had never expected the other woman to call her a friend.

Margaret Prewitt and her daughters sat in front of them on another bench a short while later. Penelope leaned forward. "Margaret, do you know my friend, Trudie?"

Margaret shook her head, turning around to smile at Trudie. "It's good to meet you. Where are you from?"

Trudie opened her mouth, but Penelope decided to answer for her. "She doesn't like to think about the past. She is focusing on the present and future."

Margaret nodded. "I think that's fine. We should all do more of that."

Trudie looked a little stunned that Penelope had jumped in to keep her from having to answer, but it obviously pleased her. "I'm looking forward to homesteading when I get to Oregon."

"Will you settle near the rest of us?" Margaret asked. "I'm hoping the men keep up these wonderful musical nights once we get there. I do miss our fiddle though." As she said the last sentence, she looked at Herb. It was a very deliberate hint that he needed to return to playing.

Herb laughed. "I promise I'll play again soon."

"You'd better," Margaret said.

Trudie smiled at the play between the others. "I would love to settle near everyone else if people want me there."

"You're wanted. If you're a friend of Penelope's, then I already feel like I can call you friend."

"Thank you," Trudie said softly.

Penelope smiled. "I'm glad that's settled. Now, Margaret, I need some help from you. What do you add to your beans to keep them from tasting like sawdust?"

Margaret smiled. "We're getting sick of beans too."

"It's so hard to keep going when that's the primary food we have to eat." Penelope wanted to groan aloud at the mere mention of beans, but as she was the one who brought them up, she didn't think that would be exactly appropriate.

"I can understand that. Here's what I do…"

Penelope took careful mental notes of everything Margaret said. She wanted to be a better cook for Herb. She wanted to be better at everything for Herb. He'd done so much for her, she had to be the best wife she could in return.

"Perhaps I could come over some evening and help you cook. I think I'd learn a lot that way if you don't mind." Penelope loved the idea of working alongside Margaret. Perhaps if she was better at cooking, it wouldn't feel like such a chore to her.

"I forgot you didn't cook before this journey. I would be very happy to teach you everything I know."

Amanda, Margaret's older daughter, turned around and looked at Penelope. "Mama's the best cook in all the world!"

Penelope laughed. "I just had someone tell me that she was going to be the best cook in all the world."

"She'll never be better than my mama." Amanda shook her head adamantly.

Margaret laughed. "She might. Maybe you should try other people's cooking."

Amanda shook her head. "No, I only want to eat yours."

"What's your favorite food?" Margaret asked Penelope.

Penelope thought about it. "Chicken and dumplings. Our cook made them for me at least once a week."

Margaret smiled. "I wonder if we could get our hands on a pullet from one of the people who brought chickens along. Or we could talk Mary into getting a bird for us. That woman could shoot anything with one hand tied behind her back and her eyes closed."

Trudie frowned. "I need to meet this Mary."

"If you haven't already, you really *do* need to," Penelope said. "She's very good at hunting, cooking, and a million other things. I'm very intimidated by her at times, but I'm so glad she taught me to shoot."

Margaret smiled. "There's no one better to teach you to shoot. I see you have your pistol on you. Have you heard anything else?"

Penelope shook her head. "I think he's probably checking the companies behind us, and he will hopefully be back after that. I don't want to think about it while we're having fun at our dance, though."

Trudie looked at her. "That man who was looking for you? You think he's coming back?"

Penelope sighed, wishing everyone would let her forget about it for the evening so she could enjoy herself. "He was sent by my father, who is angry I left. I'm sure he's coming back. My father wouldn't let him come back to Virginia without me."

"I had no idea." Trudie shook her head. "I'm so sorry."

"It's all right. I just hope I'm not putting others in danger by staying here."

"It doesn't matter if you are," Trudie said. "You're going to stay safe with us, so you can go to Oregon and open that dress shop. I love the work you did on Emily's dress."

Penelope smiled. "I'm rather proud of it. I do love to sew."

"Do you love mending?" Margaret asked.

"Of course. If I can stick a needle into it, then I love doing it."

"I may be trading some mending for some cooking lessons sometime soon then." Margaret looked excited at the prospect of avoiding her mending.

"Give me a time and I will be there."

Trudie smiled. "Not me. I can cook already."

"You can?" Penelope asked.

"I can. I'm a very good cook." Trudie shrugged. "I was a cook for a wealthy family back east for a time."

It was the most Trudie had said about her past, and Penelope filed the information away. She wanted to ask questions about it, but she knew better. If Trudie was going to stay her friend, Penelope had to accept the information she was willing to give and not ask for more.

Herb got to his feet and held his hand out for Penelope's. "I've waited while you've chattered, woman, but I'm ready for my dance with you."

Penelope got to her feet with a big smile. "As long as I get to be held in your arms, I'll be very content."

He held her hand as he led her to the "dance floor." She happily went into his arms and moved close. "In Virginia, if a couple danced this way, there were rumors she was pregnant within a week."

"Do you mind that sort of rumor?" he asked, smiling.

"Not when I'm very obviously married to you."

Beside them, Penelope noticed that girl, Edna, with her peppermint stick in her cleavage dancing some strange dance by herself. Her arms were outstretched to the sky, and she was spinning in a very odd way. Penelope liked how free she felt to be herself. She obviously hadn't been brought up with the same strict rules as Penelope had.

After the dance was over, the band played a wilder tune, and Herb surprised her by keeping her on the dance floor and continuing to dance with her. No, it wasn't a dance she'd ever heard of or seen before, but it was quite fun, and he was spinning her around in ways that had her laughing.

When they finally sat down fifteen minutes later, Trudie and Margaret were still talking. "Don't you ever dance?" Trudie asked Margaret.

Margaret smiled. "When everyone is playing, Jamie makes sure we get one dance per night. But someone hasn't been doing his share, and Jamie's had to stay up there the whole time."

Herb laughed. "You're not going to make me feel guilty for protecting my wife." He put his arm around Penelope's shoulders, hugging her to him.

Penelope smiled at their banter, glad the two of them were so comfortable talking to each other that way.

"We miss you at supper every night as well, Mr. Jensen. Your new wife is keeping you from being with the rest of the camp."

"But since my new wife is your friend, you don't mind at all, do you?"

"No, I really don't," Margaret said. "Though I wouldn't mind a dance with my husband on occasion."

Herb looked around him. "You'll both stay with Penelope? I'll go get my fiddle for one song."

Margaret looked at her friend and back at Herb. "I don't think you should leave her. I was just joking."

"I'll send Mary over."

Mary and Bob were doing a wild dance in the middle of the dancefloor as usual, and everyone was giving her a wide berth. "It might be best for everyone if you make those two sit out a dance or two," Penelope said. "Do they always dance that way?"

"They do," Margaret said as Herb hurried off to tap Bob on the shoulder and tell him what was needed.

Mary and Bob joined them and sat down. "I don't have my musket," Mary whispered.

"No, but I have your pistol," Penelope said.

"Well, give it to me so I can do my duty as protector of the weak."

"I'm not weak." Penelope wanted that to be clear. There was safety in numbers, definitely, but she didn't need to be watched over like a child.

Mary looked at Penelope and nodded. "I know you're not. I was just being silly."

Penelope introduced Mary and Trudie. "Trudie is the only other woman who was brave enough to join our company to go west with no one with her."

"Then you're not weak either," Mary said to Trudie.

"I'm aware," Trudie said. She didn't smile at Mary, but Mary didn't seem to mind.

As soon as Herb walked to the other musicians, Jamie set down his instrument and walked to Margaret. "May I have this dance, my love?"

"You may." Margaret took Jamie's hand and headed out to the middle of their makeshift dancefloor, and she went into his arms.

"I like watching Herb play," Penelope said softly to Trudie. "I've only seen him play back in Independence, but he's really good. Why am I surprised?" As far as she could tell, Herb was good at everything he did.

"I have no idea," Trudie said. "I think all of the musicians are good. I used to sit at my campfire and listen and wish people wanted me to join in the dancing."

"I don't know why you thought you weren't welcome." Penelope frowned at her friend.

"I just did," Trudie said softly. She obviously wasn't going to explain anything more, so Penelope let the subject drop.

"Margaret and Jamie look so happy dancing together, don't they?" Penelope asked.

Trudie nodded. "They do."

"They're still newlyweds," Mary said. "Sometimes it feels like half the company is newly married, and it's fun to see."

"It does, doesn't it?" Penelope asked. "It's different now that I am a newlywed and not on the outside, looking into all the fun. For a while I felt like everyone was at an exclusive party, surrounded by glass. I was allowed to look inside the party, but I wasn't allowed to enter. Not until I married anyway."

"I'm sorry we made you feel that way," Mary said. "That was never anyone's intention."

"I know it wasn't. But now that I'm married, it does feel good to be included in everything. I'm happy to be part of this big group of people who will be living together somewhere in Oregon." Penelope knew she would always have friends around her, and that's what she needed.

"I'm excited to settle in," Trudie said softly. "Do you have any idea where?"

Mary shrugged. "I have no idea about any of it. I just know we're doing it."

Penelope sighed as she watched the musicians play. Now that she was part of the group, she never wanted to leave it.

Chapter Nine

June 7th, 1852

I worry for the safety of my wife and the entire wagon train if Mr. Bradford comes back. I know everyone is doing all they can to protect Penelope, but I am not sure she can handle it if he takes her back to Virginia. I am doing all I can to keep her safe, and when I'm not with her, Mary does an admirable job of the same. I am thankful Mary took the time to teach Penelope to shoot a pistol, because I feel like she can protect herself when it is in her apron pocket.

As we cross the North Platte River, which to my understanding is the most difficult crossing of the journey, I will be busy helping everyone cross, and I won't be able to be with Penelope as much, which will worry me even more.. I have no idea what more I can do, but somehow what I am doing doesn't seem like it's nearly enough.

On the way back to their wagon from the dance, Penelope clung to Herb's arm. "I really enjoyed watching you play," she said softly. "I know I've heard you before, and I even watched you play back in Independence, but it was different tonight, knowing you're my husband. I can picture you teaching our little boys how to play the fiddle."

"Not the girls? Do you not think girls can learn to play music?" Herb grinned at her.

"Stop teasing me," she said, swatting his arm playfully. "I just picture us having a dozen little boys who all look just like you."

"That's funny, because I see us having a dozen little girls who look just like you."

She smiled. "Let's just agree to have children, and you can teach them to play. How's that?"

"Perfect," he said. "I'm setting up the tent."

"Good. I don't think I'd like making love out in the open, and after watching you play, I might have to be willing to try it." Penelope wasn't sure the most polite way to tell him she was ready to make love.

He raised an eyebrow at her. "So, you really like watching me play."

"I do! It was fun to see your passion for the music as you moved your hands over your fiddle. I felt like you were playing just for me, even though I knew better. It's hard to explain the connection I felt with you."

"Huh. Maybe I should have played the fiddle more before I was married..."

"You're not getting any husband points..."

"I'll do better." He kissed her softly. "Putting up the tent, and then we'll sleep."

Since she knew the word sleep was just a euphemism for what they were planning to do, she had no complaints. Yes, she would "sleep" with him. No problem there.

Even watching him put the tent up, his muscles flexing under his shirt as he moved the heavy wooden poles made her blood heat up. Considering she hadn't been sure she even wanted to ever marry a week ago, she was certainly taking to being a wife.

His wife.

*****

Early on Sunday morning, Herb emerged from the tent he shared with Penelope to find Mr. Bradford sitting on a rock and cooking over their fire. "May I help you?" he asked. He couldn't imagine why the man wouldn't have just stormed in and taken Penelope while he slept.

"I'm still looking for this girl, and from what I understand, she's with you. I need to take her back to Virginia." Mr. Bradford held up the portrait of Penelope. "Your wagon was pointed out as where she was staying."

As he spoke, Herb saw some of the other men in camp step forward, each of them with a gun drawn. They were ready for him to tell the truth...finally. "I married the girl you're looking for. She's my wife, and her father no longer has any hold over her. I suggest you go right back to Virginia and let him know that."

The man shook his head, reaching for the gun at his hip. "I don't recall that being in my instructions." The look Mr. Bradford gave him was menacing.

Herb nodded to the men behind the hunter. "I'm afraid you don't have a choice."

When Bradford turned, he saw fifteen barrels raised against him, and he spit. "You think you've bested me, don't you? I'll be taking that girl back to Virginia if it's the last thing I do!"

Herb sighed. "If you try again, it really will be the last thing you do." He knew no judge would convict him with so many witnesses. No, people would understand he was doing what he needed to do to protect his wife.

Bradford mounted his horse and as he rode out of camp, he called, "I'll be back."

As soon as the man was out of sight, Herb called out, "You can come out now, Penelope."

"He knows I'm here and that you're married to me. What if *you're* not safe now?" She couldn't bear the thought of losing Herb. She had finally come to the realization that she was in love with her husband, and now Mr. Bradford wanted to hurt him. She couldn't allow that to happen.

Herb shrugged. "I don't particularly care about my own safety. It's yours I'm concerned about." He ran his hands from her shoulders down to her hands.

"I..." Without another word, Penelope leaned into him and held tight. "I'm scared for both of us."

"I am too, to be honest with you, but I really don't know what to do about him. I'm going to have another meeting with the other men before church today. We'll come up with a plan to keep you safe."

She stepped back, looking up at the man she'd married, knowing that they belonged together. "Could we pay him off?" she asked. It seemed like it would be smart.

"With what? I'm *not* a rich man, Penelope." He hated to admit it, knowing what her past had been like, but he didn't have the kind of money it would take to pay the man off. Not at all.

"My jewels. I don't care about any of them but the pearls, but I'd get rid of those if it meant you'd be safer," she said softly. "None of them matter as much as you do."

"What jewels?" he asked. "I thought you gave them to Mabel before you left the plantation." He certainly hadn't seen any jewels in their wagon.

Penelope shook her head. "I gave her one ring. I have more. *So many* more." She walked to the wagon and pulled out the mostly empty flour bag where her jewelry was hidden at the bottom.

"What are you doing?" he asked, frowning.

She took the jewelry out, unwrapped it from the velvet she'd used to protect it from the flour, and laid it out for him. "I brought it all to sell to build my dress shop. I don't need any of it."

"You can't sell your jewels!" He'd never seen as much jewelry as she was showing him, and it made him a little sick to his stomach to realize that had been there without his knowledge. What if he'd thrown the sack away?

"I don't know why not. I'll never need it again. I do love the pearls my mother gave me, but nothing else even matters a little bit. So, I want to use it to have Mr. Bradford tell my family I'm dead." Penelope took a deep breath. "Father will just keep sending people until he knows I'm gone."

"I can't let you use your money. We'll find another way."

"I can't let *you* risk your life for me. This is the best way," she said softly. "It would take one necklace, and he'd do as we asked. We'd still have so many others. The only thing I care about are the pearls my mother gave me when I turned sixteen, because they belonged to her mother and her mother before her. I want to put them around the neck of my daughter when she turns sixteen. It's the only thing I'm sentimental about at all." She shrugged. "The rest are just possessions I brought along to sell when I need money."

Bob walked over from the wagon parked beside them. "I think she has a really good point. If we want to get rid of Bradford with no bloodshed, this is the answer."

Herb hated the idea with everything inside him. He wanted to be able to provide for his wife, and that meant paying off the man who was trying to kill her. "We'll talk to the others and see what everyone has to say about it," he finally said.

Penelope waited until he'd gone off with the other men before starting breakfast. Mary came over and talked to her. "I wish that man would go away and stay away."

"We all do." Penelope shook her head. "I wonder how he knew that I was in camp and with Herb."

"Someone must have told him. I don't want to think badly of anyone in our company, so I don't want to say who I think it is. No, we'll just move on as we can." Herb sighed. "I don't like this situation one bit."

Penelope sighed. "I just want him gone, so I can be happy. I found the man I want to spend the rest of my life with. This ridiculously long journey of ours is keeping us from our dream, but that man will *not*. He needs to go away, and if it takes a necklace, he can have a necklace."

Mary looked at the jewelry all laid out on the back of the wagon. "I can't believe you've had that much wealth hidden in your wagon all this time."

"Where else would I hide it? I can't put it in my pocket because my pistol's in there."

Mary laughed. "I see you're adapting quite nicely to your new circumstances, aren't you?"

"I'm trying." Penelope started cooking breakfast while Mary looked over her jewelry. "I just wish I knew exactly what to do. I mean, Herb doesn't want me to pay him off, but that seems like the smartest course of action to me."

"I don't know. I've never had anyone hunting me or had a fabulous amount of jewelry. I'm just a poor country girl. People leave me alone for the most part."

"People leave your *musket* alone," Penelope retorted. "I guess when you carry a gun everywhere you go, it doesn't feel safe to others."

"Maybe you should start carrying a musket then. That small pistol isn't nearly as frightening to look at."

Penelope laughed. "I'm glad you're here to take my mind off the danger I'm in."

"And because I'm holding a musket? So, if he comes now, he'll be scared?"

"Maybe. I wonder if it's smart for all the men to be in the same place at the same time with that man running around. It doesn't feel very safe to me," Penelope said.

"It doesn't to me either, but they're the protectors, so we should trust them." Mary grinned. "Let me show you how to make a delicious white gravy to go with your biscuits you're making for breakfast. We can put a little bit of your jerky in it, and Herb will love you forever."

"You know, I'm not sure I need to worry about making him love me forever. He already seems like he will." There was no doubt in

Penelope's mind that Herb was in love with her and that she was slowly falling in love with him.

"Still, your stomach will love you forever. Do you make gravies?"

"I do, but I've always made a dark gravy."

"This is a country gravy, and I promise you're going to be so glad you know how to do it." Mary knelt in front of the fire, showing Penelope exactly what to do. "This is going to be your new favorite for breakfast."

"I need something new for breakfast. Eggs, bacon, and johnny cakes seem to be all I've mastered."

"Then we'll teach you this, and you can cover everything else with gravy. Even if you mess things up, if they have gravy on them, people will be satisfied."

Penelope laughed. "So, I should just put gravy on everything. Even cherry cobbler?"

"Sure. He's a man. He'll love it." Mary grinned at her.

"I'm not sure how I feel about the advice you're giving me," Penelope said, shaking her head.

"Maybe you only listen to a little piece of it."

*****

Herb left the meeting with the men of the company feeling dejected. Almost everyone agreed that Penelope should just pay Bradford to pretend she was dead, but Herb didn't like that solution. He wanted the man gone, but he didn't want Penelope to have to part with any of her jewelry.

As he and Bob headed back to their respective wagons, Bob said, "I really do think it makes the most sense. And she seemed more than willing to do it. Just let her take care of it that way, and then no lives need to be lost."

Herb nodded. "I guess that's what we'll do. I hate it though."

"I know."

When Herb got back to Penelope, he told her what had been decided. "I guess if you're willing to actually pay the man to tell your father you're dead, that's what you should do. I hate the idea, but I've been outvoted."

Penelope offered him biscuits, eggs, and gravy. "I'm sorry you hate the solution so much, but it feels like the only thing we can do. You were telling me just the other day how important human life is. This will keep any lives from being lost."

"That's true," he said softly. "I really don't like the idea of anyone dying, and if we kill Bradford, other men will just be sent to look for you."

"They will. My father is not going to give up."

"I wouldn't either if you went missing. You're too precious."

She smiled. "Thank you."

After the church service he worked on several wagons, and then after supper, they went for one of their walks. As they walked, he explained the plans for the next day. "It was also decided today that the river is low enough for us to cross tomorrow. We're going to float the wagons across, and then we'll use the canoes that were left here by those who have gone before us so the people can cross. It's still going to be dangerous, but we hope it won't be so dangerous that we lose anyone to the river."

She nodded. "And you'll be helping with the removal of the wheels?" She wanted him to be doing the safest job available.

"I will be overseeing it for every wagon. We'll spend the entire day getting everyone across, and it could even take two days. Then we'll put the wagons back together. I want you staying with Mary through it all."

"Of course, I will. You know I've been really cautious through this whole ordeal."

Herb nodded. "You have. I'm just so afraid I'm going to lose you."

Penelope went into his arms and leaned into him. "You're not going to lose me, because I want to be found. By you. Only by you."

*****

The following day was the most hectic they'd had on the trail. Herb ate breakfast and immediately helped the lead wagon get ready to cross the river, while Penelope was still washing the breakfast dishes. Once she'd stowed the dishes away, she was careful to follow Herb's instructions exactly and get everything tied down the way he said.

While she worked at that, she could see Mary doing the same in the wagon next to hers, and Mary seemed to be watching every move she made. When Penelope finished her task, she walked over to help Mary finish up. "I see you watching me, and I thank you for it. Herb is really afraid to be away from me today."

"I feel better when you're within sight. I think Herb's paranoia is rubbing off on me."

"I can see why," Penelope said as she tied the last knot to secure Mary's wagon. "Let's help Trudie next."

Mary nodded. "Your friend is a bit odd. I'm not sure what I think of her yet."

"Give her time. She's frightened of something, and she hasn't found a way to open up about it."

They helped Trudie, and then worked their way around the camp, helping all the others get their wagons and goods secure to be floated across the river.

When it was time for the noon meal, Penelope was glad she'd kept out what they had left of the meal she'd made the night before. It was only biscuits and gravy with jerky cut up in it, but Herb had really enjoyed it. He'd loved it so much the previous morning, that she'd made it for supper as well. It was easy, and it pleased him, and those two things were the most important to Penelope.

They ate from the same pot because Penelope had already secured the dishes, but it was still a good meal. "How's it going?" she asked Herb.

"It's going much faster than expected, thanks to two women who walked around the whole camp helping others get their wagons secure. It's taking so many men to take wagons apart and float them across, that there was no one to spare. If the wagons had come to us unsecured, we'd have to take the time to check each rope and make sure they were as they needed to be. Now, we're able to just float them."

"Oh, good," Penelope said. "Mary and I tried to make sure everyone was ready to go as soon as they could be."

"You two did a great job." He ate his last bite and stood up. "Back to it. We have less than half of the wagons across so far, and if we want to finish today, that means a long day. But it also means we can probably get everything reassembled in the morning, and we can start out after noon. I think we'll all feel safer as we get more and more land between us and Bradford."

"No one has seen him today," Penelope said softly. "Mary and I have been watching and asking everyone."

"Good. Keep your eyes peeled and make sure you have your pistol with you and ready." Herb kissed her forehead as he headed back to the task at hand.

Penelope scrubbed her pot out down near the river, and as she was walking back toward camp, a hand clamped over her mouth, pulling her away from the others. "Don't make a sound. You hear me?"

Penelope nodded, glad she was still wearing her apron. He would never guess she was armed, and she would just need to wait for the right moment to use her pistol. She was determined that it was all going to be fine, and she would see Herb again within a few hours. And then she started praying.

*****

Herb was working on getting one of the wheels off the Bedwells' wagon when Mary came up to him, looking frantic. "I haven't seen Penelope since lunchtime. I thought she was probably just taking care of necessities, and she'd be back at any moment, but she wasn't. It's been an hour."

Herb stood up, his eyes wide. "An hour? And you're just now telling me?" He wanted to shake Mary, but that wasn't his place. No, his job now was to find his wife and find her fast.

"I'm so sorry! I feel like I've fallen down on the job."

He rubbed his hand over his face. "It's not your fault. With the chaos the camp is in today, it was the perfect time for him to make his move."

Mary frowned. "What are we going to do?"

"You're going to go back to camp and let the other women know that she's gone. She might still be somewhere in camp and you just don't realize it."

Mary looked skeptical, but she hurried back toward the camp. As soon as she was gone, Herb called to the other men. "It looks like Penelope's been taken. I'm going to get one of her necklaces and try to negotiate with the man."

"I'm going with you," Bob said, immediately moving to Herb's side.

Malcolm nodded. "You may need a doctor."

"We can't all go!" Herb said.

"Well, no more can really be done here without a blacksmith," Bedwell said, "so we may as well all go and see if we can find your lost wife."

Behind Bedwell was a large splashing sound, and Herb turned to see a small girl go under the water. He couldn't tell who it was, and he knew someone had to take care of her, but he needed to get his wife. Penelope had to take precedence. There were others to help the girl.

Bedwell was the first to jump into the water, and he went after the child. While he was taking care of the girl, and two others were helping him, Herb instructed men to go in every direction looking for Penelope. They had to find her.

He barely noticed as the girl came out of the water, but Bedwell was nowhere to be seen. He'd find out what happened later. He ran to camp to get one of the necklaces while Bob saddled horses for them.

He took one of his horses and with Bob at his side—the doctor had to stay to help the girl—they were on their way. They rode back the way the company had come, east along the river.

He knew Bradford would have Penelope on his horse with him, because he hadn't had another, and they should be able to overtake him quickly if this was the direction they'd gone.

*****

Penelope struggled on the horse, biting down hard on Mr. Bradford's filthy hand. As soon as he let go, she let out a loud scream she hoped would be heard. He stopped the horse and dismounted, dragging her off with him. "You're going to behave. I'm not having you fight me the whole way back to Virginia."

"The only way you'll get me to Virginia is to kill me first," she spat at him. "I'm not going back. Do you know what Reginald Black is like?"

"I don't care what he's like. You're going to Virginia with me, and I'm taking you to your father, who better pay me extra for my troubles. How did you hide so well?"

"I'm married. They don't *want* me back!" she said. "Reginald wants a woman as pure as the driven snow, and I'm not that any longer."

"Then I guess it doesn't matter if I have a little fun with you along the way," he said, reaching for his belt buckle.

Penelope had managed to free her hands from the ropes he'd tied around her wrists, and one hand immediately went into her apron pocket. "I don't think you're going to have any fun with me at all," she said calmly, pulling back the hammer.

He stared at her. "You're bluffing. You can't possibly know how to use that thing. You're a soft southern woman."

"You have me confused with someone else, Mr. Bradford. I assure you, all softness went out of me the day my father sold my best friend. You have two options right now. I can shoot you, which really would be my preference at this point, or you can make a deal with me. I'll give you a diamond necklace my father gave me when I first came out, and you'll go back to Virginia and tell my father I died. Either way, I win. If you take the necklace, then you can win with me."

He looked surprised for a moment. "You may know how to shoot, but you wouldn't kill me."

She aimed carefully for his shoulder as he rushed toward her and pulled the trigger. Her aim was true, and he grasped the spot where the bullet slammed into him and fell to the ground. "I shot you, but I didn't kill you. There's another bullet in this gun, and if you don't lie there quietly, I will use it."

Penelope surprised even herself as she stood there over him with the gun pointed at him. She'd been unsure whether or not she could ever shoot anyone, but she hadn't hesitated. She didn't want to kill him, but she knew in that moment if she had to, she'd do it without hesitation.

Bradford lay on the ground, clutching his shoulder. "Your father underestimated you."

"He always has."

*****

Herb heard a gunshot from up ahead and he spurred his horse to go faster. He could picture Penelope lying on the ground, and he had to get the image out of his head.

Bob yelled at him. "Herb, stop!"

"I can't! She may be hurt. She may be dead!" He was frantic to get to his wife. He had to know she was all right.

"You're not going to help either of you if you rush into the situation without thinking first. Stop for a minute."

Herb knew his friend was right, and he pulled back on the reins stopping the horse. "I don't know what I'm going to do if he killed her."

"Okay, we can't both go barreling in from the same directly. Give me five minutes and I'll ride out wide, then come in at an angle. We're going to be sure she's all right." Bob looked at Herb. "Do you have the necklace?"

"Yes of course. I'm scared for my wife, but it hasn't turned me into an idiot."

Bob nodded. "All right. Give me a little time, and we'll both start riding toward the gunshot in five minutes. All right?"

Herb nodded his agreement, and sat atop his horse, waiting as Bob moved into position. He was glad there was someone cool-headed with him because all he could think about was saving his wife.

As he sat there, he tried to come up with the names they would give the children they would have when he found her, and she was safe. He knew it was a silly thing to do, but it kept his mind off his worries. "Josephine, Ruby, Lillian, Dean, Roy, Linda, Vicki..."

He ran out of names as he sat in shock, thinking about what had happened. The woman he loved more than all others—more than he'd ever dreamed he could love anyone—had been taken from him and was lying on the ground, hurt.

What if she was bleeding out as he sat there coming up with names for children they would never have? What if she couldn't survive, because he wasted so much time?

But he knew Bob was right, and he'd only put her in more danger by rushing in without at least thinking about it first. Surely it had been five minutes. It had to have been.

He counted to sixty, and then he started riding toward the sound of the gunshot. Toward his wife and his entire future. Toward the only woman he had ever loved.

She had to be all right. He couldn't let himself dwell on the possibility of her being hurt or dead. He wouldn't be able to do what he needed to do, unless he was sure she was standing there with her pistol in her hand, so that's what he decided he was riding toward.

Penelope was going to be found, and he was just going to her to give her a ride back to camp so they could continue their journey to Oregon. So, all could be perfect with their lives, and they could live happily ever after. She'd once told him that she dreamed of happily ever after, so that's what they were going to have.

Someday they would be sitting in Oregon, in beautifully carved rocking chairs, and their grandchildren would be playing around them. And they would tell their grandchildren the story of going west on the Oregon Trail and how someone had kidnapped their grandmother.

It was a story no one else would be telling their grandchildren, and he knew it would be true.

Herb knew that his love was waiting for him, and he was going to find her.

Chapter Ten

Monday, June 8th, 1852

It seems that the danger is gone. I feel like a weight has been lifted off my shoulders. Mr. Bradford accepted our bribe of one of my necklaces to go back to Virginia and tell my father I'm dead. He will be recovering from the bullet wound I gave him along the way.

It's true. I actually used my pistol on a human, and I saved myself when I was kidnapped. I never thought I could actually do it, but I did.

I left Virginia in February, a young lady who had been sheltered from many things while at the same time experiencing the horrors of having a friend torn from her and killed. Now, I'm a strong independent woman. I didn't have to wait for Herb to save me, though he arrived shortly after I shot Mr. Bradford, and it did help that he had my necklace, but I still saved myself. In my story, the heroine saved herself and the hero rode in after she'd done so.

I've always loved fairy tales, because the hero saves the heroine. Now, I will be able to teach my daughters that sometimes the heroine must save herself to get to her happily ever after. As I have done.

Penelope looked up as she heard two horses riding toward her, but she never took the gun off Mr. Bradford. She wasn't going to let him get the upper hand again. When she saw Herb, she smiled. "It's nice of you to come and help me."

Herb's grin was a mile wide as he dismounted and walked toward her. "Do not take your gun off him."

"I wouldn't. He did say he would be amenable to our bribe. He'll take the necklace and go back to father and report my death on the trail."

Herb stood beside Penelope, realizing that he could see Bob riding toward them. "You will?"

Mr. Bradford nodded. "I need a doctor."

"It looks like she did a good job. Did the bullet go clean through or is it lodged in there somewhere?"

Bradford's face went white. "I haven't checked."

"Maybe I should do that for you," Herb said, liking the idea of probing the man's shoulder with the knife he carried.

"No! Just get me to a doctor."

Herb sighed. "How do you want this scum to tell your father you died, wife?"

Penelope considered. "I could die of cholera, but that is such a dreadful disease. I don't want to die that way. I suppose I could drown...or be trampled by a herd of buffalo. You know what? I like that one. Tell Father I was trampled by a herd of buffalo, all right, Mr. Bradford?"

"Whatever you want, Miss Brainerd."

Penelope glared at the injured man. "My name is Mrs. Jensen."

"Yes, Mrs. Jensen. So sorry to forget." Bradford seemed afraid of Penelope and Herb wanted to laugh. His Southern belle of a wife had become a strong, pioneer woman, and he couldn't be prouder of her.

Herb pulled a necklace from his shirt pocket. "Will this one work?"

"That one will work beautifully," Penelope said.

Bradford's eyes widened. "Are those real diamonds?" he asked.

"Of course, they are. What do you take me for?" Penelope asked. "I'm offended you doubt the authenticity of my diamonds. I want to kick him now, Herb. May I kick him? Or do you want to do it?"

Herb laughed. "Let's leave Bob here to watch over him and tell the doc how to find him. I want to get you back to camp."

"Where I'm safe?" she asked, her eyes twinkling.

"I think we all underestimated you," Herb said, shaking his head. "I always knew you were a strong woman, but you have outshone even my wildest expectations."

"You need to remember this," Penelope said. "I can shoot now, and I don't want to have to use this pistol on you."

Herb laughed, his arm going around his wife. "I'm so proud of you."

She grinned. "I did it. I saved myself."

"I probably should have just let you handle things from the very beginning," he said.

"You should have." Penelope looked at Mr. Bradford. "My friend Bob is going to keep a gun on you until the doctor gets here, but then you're on your own. Do you understand that? You're not coming back to camp to recover. You will be on your way, or I'll shoot you again."

"I will be on my way." Bradford yelped as the necklace hit his chest. "Your father will believe you were trampled by a herd of buffalo. I swear it."

Penelope handed Bob her gun. "If he causes trouble, you'll need to shoot him again. He doesn't much care for being shot."

"I can't imagine why," Bob said, a huge grin on his face. "Make sure Mary knows I'm all right, and I'll be back soon. And tell her what an amazing job she did teaching you to shoot."

She smiled. "I sure will."

Bradford groaned. "You mean a woman taught another woman to shoot? Don't you men know how to control the ladies around here?"

Bob laughed. "My lady is impossible to control, and that's what I love best about her."

Herb took Penelope's hand and led her back to his horse. "Do you know how to ride?" he asked.

"No, but I really want to learn. I think I want to be able to do anything you can do."

"I'm not going to teach you to blacksmith, but only because we only need one blacksmith in town. We need a dressmaker too."

"I guess that's true." She sighed happily. "I did a good job, didn't I?"

"You did." He mounted the horse and held a hand down for her. "Step on my foot and swing up behind me."

"How? I don't have a side saddle!"

He chuckled. "Lady, you just shot a man, threatened to kick him, and then told him you'd shoot him again if you saw him again. I think you can ride astride just this once."

"I suppose I can, but it's not nearly as ladylike." She did as he'd instructed, standing on his foot and swinging up behind him. She had to bunch her skirts up a little so she could sit astride, but she did it, and then she wrapped her arms around him. "I'm so glad that's over."

Herb nodded. "You have no idea what went through my mind when I heard that gunshot."

"I'm sorry for the fright it must have given you, but...I'm not sorry for the way it turned out." She frowned. "Oh, no. Are all the wagons going to be able to cross today with you gone for so long?"

He chuckled. "I don't think anyone is as worried about crossing that river as they are about you coming back to camp safe and sound."

"Really?" she asked. "I'm surprised."

"Oh, I just remembered one of the girls fell into the river just before I left to find you. They got her out, but I didn't see Bedwell before I left."

"Mr. Bedwell?" she asked. "What does he have to do with anything?"

"Believe it or not, he saw her fall and jumped in after her. I think he got her out, but I'm not sure. There were hands there helping, and I was focused on finding you."

Penelope blinked. "So, I was saved, but Mr. Bedwell may have died?" As much as she didn't like Bedwell, she felt bad that she had taken some of the men who could help save him away when he needed them.

"I don't know if he died or not. I really didn't take the time to see."

"I'll pray for him the whole way back to camp."

Herb sighed. "I heard how he treated you the day you both had supper with the Bentleys. Why are you praying for him?" He wasn't sure he could bring himself to pray for Bedwell after how he'd treated Penelope. So, how could she?

"Because I was taught to pray for my enemies. And I don't think Mr. Bedwell is an enemy. He's just an angry, misguided man. He deserves a chance to be happy, don't you think?"

"I guess everyone does."

The whole way back he heard her mumbling her prayer. Sometimes she prayed for the little girl who fell into the water, sometimes for Bedwell, and he even heard Bradford's name mentioned a time or two. It made no sense to him that she was that concerned about people who had hurt her, and a little girl whose identity she didn't know, but it was who she was. A wonderful, sweet woman who cared about others more than she cared about herself.

A girl who had left a life of ease so she could go west and never have anything to do with slavery. A woman whom he loved with everything inside him. The woman who he would have children with and spend the rest of his life loving.

As soon as they got back to camp, they found the doctor, who had been ministering to Mr. Bedwell. "He sucked too much water into his lungs," Dr. Bentley said. "If he doesn't die from pneumonia, it'll be a miracle."

Penelope noticed Katie standing beside the doctor. "I'll watch over him. He saved my little girl."

Penelope hurried to her friend. "It was your daughter who fell into the river? She's all right?" She put her arm around Katie, knowing she must have been frantic for the time her daughter was in the water.

"She is. Mr. Bedwell fished her out of the water, and then he was caught by the current and forced under. Some of the other men got him out, but we're not sure if he's going to be all right. He hasn't woken up yet."

Herb frowned. "Doc, I need you to go and see to the man Penelope shot. She got him in the shoulder. I'd say let's let him die, but he's going to go back to Virginia, and tell her father that she's dead."

"I chose to die being trampled by a herd of buffalo," Penelope added.

Katie smiled at her. "I think that's a very good choice. You go quickly that way with no suffering."

The doctor stood. "Of course, I'll go with you, Herb. Let's get that man bandaged up, and then I can come back and sit with Bedwell."

"No need," Katie said. "I'll stay for as long as I need to."

"Thank you," Dr. Bentley said, grabbing his medical bag and following Herb from camp.

"How can I help you, Katie?" Penelope asked.

"After what you've been through, I don't think you should be asking me that."

"Well, I am. Could I get supper for your children?"

Katie frowned and nodded. "Please. Maybe farm the children out to others so that I can keep caring for the man who risked his own life for my little girl. And his children! Don't forget someone needs to watch his boys!"

"I won't," Penelope said as she hurried from the tent they'd set up for the sick man.

When she got out, she did everything Katie had requested, and then she found some of the last money she had saved from the sale of one of her necklaces and bought a chicken from one of the other women in camp. "I'm going to make some chicken soup," she said to herself, and immediately Margaret was beside her.

"I'll help you with the soup, and Jamie and I will watch over Katie's little girl while she helps Mr. Bedwell." Margaret shook her head. "I never thought I'd say it, but I'm praying for him. He did something really good here, and I don't think he should be punished for it."

"Neither do I. I never thought we'd see good in Mr. Bedwell, but here we are, trying to save his life after he saved a little girl from drowning. Maybe there's good in him after all."

"There must be, because from the way I hear it, he just jumped in after the child, giving no thought to his own safety. He's not the man any of us thought he was."

Penelope nodded, thinking about her own experience with the bitter man. "I pray he's all right."

Margaret looked at her. "In thinking about the former captain, I forgot to ask how you got away."

"And I forgot to tell you." Penelope smiled. "It's a good story. I'll be talking to my grandchildren about it someday." She briefly explained pulling the pistol and Mr. Bradford telling her she would never use it, and his shock when she had. "I told him if he ever comes around our camp, I'd shoot him again, and he didn't seem to like that idea."

Margaret laughed. "I should say he didn't. I'm so glad you're fine."

"To me, it's more than being fine. Three months ago, I was a Southern Belle engaged to a man my father chose, who I knew my life would be miserable with. Now I'm a strong woman who rescued herself from the man who kidnapped her. Even a week ago, I wouldn't have believed it was possible."

"That's a wonderful story."

"Now you have to know to teach your girls that sometimes the heroine doesn't have to wait for the hero. Sometimes she has to rescue herself."

Margaret nodded. "I do think I'll let you tell them the story the next time we move on. I have a feeling we might stay in place for a day or two to give Mr. Bedwell time to heal. After everything, I still want to call him the captain, and I have no idea why."

"I know what you mean. That's how we all first met him, and it seems inappropriate to call him anything else."

"Exactly," Margaret said.

Margaret spent the next hour showing Penelope how to butcher and remove the feathers from a chicken prior to boiling it.

As soon as the bird was in the pot, they gathered carrots and potatoes and seasoning to make the broth better. They were both surprised at the number of people who were willing to share some of their food for the soup.

By the time they were done, there was a huge pot of soup roasting over a fire, and Penelope looked downriver, hoping to see Herb, Bob, and the doctor coming toward them.

When they finally came into sight, she breathed a sigh of relief. They were all safe and it was truly over. Mr. Bradford was done searching for her, and as soon as he was done licking his wounds, he'd be off to Virginia to speak with her father. She was safe, and so were the people she loved.

She ran to Herb and held onto him as he dismounted, pleased to have him back safely. "Margaret and I are making a huge pot of soup, and that's what we're having for supper," she finally said as she pulled away.

"I'm not exactly worried about what our supper will be," he said, but his stomach chose that moment to growl, proving him a liar. "Well, not *too* worried anyway."

After they'd done the supper dishes and checked on the former captain once more, Herb said the words she loved to hear. "Take a walk with me."

Together, they left the camp and walked along the river. "This will be our last night on this side of the river," he said. He pointed to the other side, where several of the families were already camped.

Edna stood across the river and waved happily at them.

Penelope waved back with a smile on her face. "I like her," she said.

"Edna? She's strange, but I do believe she's going to be a wonderful mother someday."

"I think so too." As they walked, she thought about how she wanted to say what she had to tell him. Did just coming out with it work best, or should she lead into it so as not to stun him. "I had a lot of time to think today."

"So, did I," he said softly. "When I heard that gunshot, I was certain you were dead, and I was racing toward you, but Bob made me stop and think about what to do, and it really helped. I had to picture you alive so that I could keep going. So, I pictured us as an old married couple, with our grandchildren all around us. We talked to them about how their grandmother rescued herself."

She smiled. "I've had those same thoughts today, but I also had a more important thought."

"You did? What was more important than my future grandchildren?" he asked.

She laughed. "I realized as I was waiting for you to come get me, and I never had a moment's doubt that you would, that I love you. With everything inside me. You are the man I've waited my whole life to have God bring to me, and here you are. I don't know why I didn't realize it until today. I guess I was just so blind, thinking about the danger..."

He spun her toward him and kissed her deeply. "I love you right back, Penelope. I've wanted to tell you for such a long time, but I didn't want to scare you away. I know you married me simply because of the danger you were in, but that's not why I married you. I married you because from the first time I heard your southern drawl I knew that I needed to have you in my life for the rest of my days. You are the one I want to grow old with. The one I want to make memories with. The one I want to love forever."

She smiled up at him. "I'm almost glad for the crazy week of danger I was in, because I don't know if I'd have been able to see past my nose to the most wonderful man in the world without that prompting. I think I must have been blind."

He hugged her close. "You're my everything, Penelope. I hope you know that I wouldn't trade a minute with you for all the riches in the world, though I now feel like we have all the riches in the world with the jewelry you have hidden in a flour sack of all places."

She laughed. "I had some friends whose husbands sold their jewelry as soon as they married, and I didn't want you to be tempted."

"Oh, I wasn't tempted. Not at all. But now I know that we can give beautiful jewelry to our daughters."

"Or we can sell them and build a blacksmith shop and a dress shop. Maybe we could have them next to each other, and you could come to the shop and eat with me at noon."

He smiled. "I like the thought of that. What about when the children come? Where will they be while you're at the dress shop?"

"Maybe we could find a former slave to come and we'll pay her to watch them. I don't know. We'll worry about that when the time comes."

"Yes, we will. For now, let's just worry about how much we love each other, and how we're going to finish crossing that river..."

She sighed. "And whether or not the captain will survive."

"The former captain," Herb said, frowning. "I hate to think of him lying there so ill."

"So, do I, but I think if he was going to get sick, he did it for all the right reasons."

"Maybe there's good in him after all. We may never have known without that danger today."

"No, we wouldn't have." She rested her head on his shoulder. "We're going to make it to Oregon and have those children, aren't we?"

"Did you doubt it?"

"Not for a minute."

Sign up for instant notification of all of Kirsten's new releases. Text 'BOB' to 42828 to sign up for her email newsletter.

and

For a complete list of Kirsten's works head to her website kirstenosbourne.com[1]

---

www.ingramcontent.com/pod-product-compliance
Lightning Source LLC
Chambersburg PA
CBHW031422150726
47989CB00002B/750